THE ELVEN SPYMASTER'S THIEF

ELVES OF ELDARLAN - BOOK ONE

The Elven Spymaster's Thief

Elves of Eldarlan
Book One

Elisa Rae

ISBN: 9798795986616

Cover by Rossano Designs

One

Avril

My master, the Warlord Grimore, was crazed. I surveyed the home of my target with a sinking stomach. Spymaster Whispier was notorious for knowing everything. Nothing remained safe from him and his minions. He commanded the largest host of shadow elves in all of the Eldarlan. Nothing was above or beneath his notice—well, except me. And I wanted to keep it that way. Being known by this elf was dangerous.

For most of my life, ever since my brother was trapped into the mastermind's service, I had been avoiding the elf's notice. I had kept myself beneath his notice for years by not speaking of things that he might wish to know, not moving in circles close to him, and avoiding any mission that had any possibility of brushing his purview. It proved a solid approach to keeping distance between us, until now.

Sadly, my will wasn't completely my own, and my master wanted something of Whispier's, something located close to his person. It was an item he kept with him at all times. As I regarded the sprawling palace before me, I struggled to calm the nerves twisting my gut. This was the point of no return. After this, the most powerful elf in the northern elven realm would know my work and have a reason to track me down.

Enough ruminating—I shook myself from my worries. This was not time for distraction. The glow of the magical lights floating about the expansive gardens surrounding the palace intensified in brightness as the last blaze of sunset faded from the western sky. It was time to move.

Pulling my magic hood, a recent gift from a grateful brownie, over my face, I blinked in the sudden darkness.

"Stealth," I whispered.

My vision cleared as the spell quickly adjusted to the darkness. I glanced around, adapting to the vision change. Darkness brightened, and shadows revealed all their secrets. Among the plants, a shadow elf leaped from shadow to shade, blinking in and out of existence as he jumped from dark spot to dark spot on his journey around the palace.

I shivered. Being caught by a wraithwalking elf was death.

Finally, the sun was truly gone and the floating lights along the paths began to fade. I watched the palace. Surely that was a sign that the occupants were preparing for sleep. Fewer servants meant fewer chances of being caught.

Two hours later, the wraithwalking elf hadn't returned. I slipped out of my hiding place and began making my way toward the balcony that my gathered intel indicated led to Whispier's study. As I approached, I eyed the intricately carved columns framing the edifice and supporting the overhanging stone and metal. Covered with climbing ivy, they appeared deceptively easy to climb. I hesitated.

Edging the vines aside, I found exactly what I feared. Razor wire laced with detection spells draped beneath the camouflage. It would've sliced through my boots, cutting the bottoms of my feet to ribbons. I replaced the vines and retreated to the hedge across the path from the balcony.

Pressing my back into the leafy depths of a generous bush, I scanned the face of the building. As confident as I was in the look-away charm on my cloak, I didn't have faith enough to rely on it alone to keep alert eyes from seeing me. Besides, I hadn't tested it on elves yet. Until this very mission, I had never even ventured into the kingdom of Eldralan.

Elegantly arched windows of flawless glass reflected the dim glow of the floating lights, creating opaque surfaces and hiding the rooms beyond. The glittery sheen flickered subtly across some of the panes but not others.

The door beneath the balcony wasn't spelled. Strange, but it wasn't prohibitively so. I suspected it was at least locked. Also, elves were notorious for their overconfidence in their mystique. I didn't wish to test that reputation. But one must do what one must.

I adjusted the hood's fit around my head and checked that my cloak still covered both of my shoulders as the brownie indicated it should for full protection. Rising from the depths of the bush, I slipped across the stone pavers to the door.

The lock, though sophisticated, was just that, a lock. No magic, no alarms, so nothing I couldn't handle. Edging the door open a crack, I scoped out a potential hiding spot behind a great fern just inside the entrance and to the left. Slipping through, I eased the door closed while scanning the room, and then silently moved behind the covering foliage.

I peered through the feathery leaves of my hiding place in disgust. Plants, flowers, and vines crowded the walls. To top it all off, there was an entire tree planted in the center of the room. It wasn't a small tree either. The branches completely obscured the ceiling, and to make it even odder, the fruit glowed.

Hushed footfalls of someone approaching snapped my attention to the open doorway across the room.

"Do you require anything else this evening, Master Whispier?" A tall elf, slender even for his species, dressed in a long tunic and leather leggings of medium gray, bowed to someone out of sight. I could just make out his profile and clothing through the opening into the main house.

"Send Casimir to me when he returns from his rounds. Then I shall retire for the evening," a male voice replied from somewhere to the right of the door. "That is all."

"Very well." The elf in gray bowed before moving almost soundlessly off to the left.

Inwardly groaning at the prospect of waiting even longer for the household to settle in for the night, I listened. Master Whispier ascended the stairs to the second floor and then entered the room above me, the very room I needed to search first.

Scanning the room for a better hiding place, I found one behind a rather large berry bush to the right of the open door. Crouching there, I listened for movement above me.

For a supposedly light-footed elf, Master Whispier made quite a bit of noise. Time passed. Then, the movement of a wraithwalker passed through the glass wall behind me. One moment he was a whispy, dark form beneath the balcony and just visible through the unspelled windows. The next, he stood beneath the tree in the center of the room. Only the sudden cropping up of goosebumps on my flesh warned me.

I swallowed a gasp of surprise and froze. My heartbeat thundered so loudly in my ears I swore he must've heard it. Did elves have superior hearing as well as all their other blessed attributes? For a brief moment, I feared they did.

The shadow elf, an inky outline against the glow of the lights in the garden, hesitated. Tilting his opaque head, his black profile outlined against the fogged glass, he appeared to listen. My traitorous heartbeat grew louder and more frantic. I held my breath in an effort to slow it.

Then, as suddenly as he appeared, he was gone. The swift movement and soft whump of displaced air passed next to me, tickling the exposed skin between my sleeve and the glove of my left hand. The tingling traces of elf magic flickered against my cheek.

"Casimir," Master Whispier said above my head. "Report."

The shadow elf replied, but his words were obscured. Whispier's reply took on the same muffled quality, making me fear I had been discovered. Had the shadow elf seen me? Was that why they disguised their words? Because he knew I was eavesdropping? But then, why leave me here?

About an hour passed, and still, they murmured back and forth. I abandoned the idea of my possible discovery for the idea that they were just paranoid. It fit the intel better.

Leaning my head back against the wall, I lifted my hand to my face to rub my forehead before I remembered my hood. Dropping my hand once again, I eyed the blurred sky beyond the garden. How long did it take to deliver a report?

Then suddenly, the voices ceased. A soft whump next to me and then beneath the tree marked the exit of the shadow elf. According to the diagrams I had memorized, the footfalls above retreated toward the spymaster's bed chamber in one of the adjoining rooms. I almost groaned with relief. Let him fall to sleep quickly. Then I could claim the prize and get out of this dangerous palace.

I remained in my hiding place another half hour by my reckoning before moving through the open door into the next room. It was twice the breadth of the plant room and twice as tall. Instead of a tree crowding the ceiling, a huge dome made of cut and stained glass twinkled in the glow of a dim floating globe. I had stumbled into the front entrance. A sweeping staircase hugged the wall from the excessively tall double doors opposite me to above my head where it passed before my first destination, the door into Spymaster Whispier's study.

Within minutes, I crept up the stairs and reached the door. Placing my ear to the wood, I listened. Nothing but the rushing sound of my own blood in my ears.

I tried the handle. To my utter astonishment, it turned. A chill pricked my skin. What spymaster worth his reputation neglected to lock his study?

A soft thump came from the foyer below.

I never moved through a doorway so fast in my life. By some miracle, I managed to close it behind me without making a sound. Only once the latched clicked in place did I pause to assess the room I had entered.

Elegant but masculine furniture adorned with a minimum of decoration lined the walls. A single expansive table dominated the center of the room. In a place of honor, sitting literally in the middle of that enormous slab of polished wood, was the very object I had been sent to retrieve.

The moment my eyes fell on the dagger, I knew something was very wrong. The thing was ugly, roughly made, and hardly even functional. Why did my master send me into the den of the greatest mastermind in Eldarlan to steal a child's toy? I squinted at it. It was not even an enchanted toy.

Still, I had my orders. My life and livelihood depended on fulfilling this mission. Grimore wouldn't tolerate anything less than absolute success. Letting out the smallest of silent sighs, I approached the table. I ascertained that it hadn't been boobytrapped either magically or otherwise using all of my observational skills.

Well, here I go, I thought. I reached across the table and lifted the small dagger from its display.

"Are you sure you want that one?"

I jumped. My heart threatened to leap from my chest. For one frantic moment, I feared I would die from fright. I whirled toward the voice. Anger replaced panic in an instant. "Are you trying to kill me?"

"No." He was lean, but there was a substance to his frame, unlike most elves I had seen from afar. Muscle across the chest and shoulders gave his long lines a dangerous power that had nothing to do with magic. His piercing green eyes assessed me with a sharpness that made me want to flinch away. Unlike most of his kind, he had cropped his brown hair instead of letting it flow down his back. The tapered curls did nothing to hide the pointed tips of his ears. His clothing also had a simpler cut, but the fabric was no less fine. It hung in appealingly elegant lines, accentuating his feline-like movements as he stalked across the hardwood floor. "I was merely curious."

"Whether or not you could shock my heart into stopping?" I backed up until my hips hit the edge of the table behind me. I still clutched the sheathed dagger to my chest. After all this, I had no intention of leaving without it.

"Human hearts are fragile, but I have never known one as young as yours to stop due to shock. Blade, curse, poison, draining, or ripping it from the chest, yes. Those can kill, but fright, no." He held out his elegant hand. "Give me the blade."

"No." Unnerved by how unfailingly he stared into my eyes despite my bespelled cloak and the mask obscuring my features. Attraction warred with the fission of alarm.

"I could take it by force."

"You will lose more than you gain in the process."

His impassive features moved. An eyebrow rose slightly as though intrigued. "I am stronger than I look."

I snorted. "So am I." I slid my favorite blade from its hiding place without letting go of the useless one I was trying to steal. There was no way this thug of Whispier's was going to relieve me of my prize, elf or not.

In an instant, before I could react, a long thin stiletto flicked into his fingers, and the cool edge of the blade rested against my throat. "I am faster."

"That may be," I admitted.

A twitch near his eye broke through his stoic mask. "But?"

I leaned slightly back from his blade, giving me the ability to swallow. His eyes narrowed as he watched the movement of my throat. I used the distraction wisely.

"Speed isn't everything." I pressed the edge of my deadly iron-laced blade to his gut, perfectly positioned to drive it straight up into his stomach at the slightest provocation.

To my surprise, the corner of his mouth twitched, and he stepped closer. "I doubt you will have time to follow through on that threat. A quick flick of my wrist, and you will be dead in seconds."

I stared into the mysterious depths of his enigmatic spring green eyes. He was close enough that I could see the blue flecks near his pupil and the ring of silver around the iris' outer edge. I could also feel him. His deep, even breaths fluttered against the mask, bringing the scents of trees, fresh air, and the promise of something inexplicable. A tingle of wild magic different from the comfortable brownie charms on my cloak invaded my head. A sleep spell! It whispered sweetly of warmth and comfort, tempting me to relax.

I closed my eyes. Abruptly the sensation ceased. I jabbed my knife into his gut, not hard enough to break the skin, but enough to get him to back up ever so slightly.

"Your death will be more painful," I growled as I opened my eyes to glare at him. The spell was still there, trying to invade my head again. However, now that I was aware of it, I could resist it.

"I will heal." Something changed in his eyes.

"But you will suffer while you heal." I frowned. What had changed in his eyes? Laughter? "You are laughing at me!" I shoved at his chest hard. He complied, but the way he did it—moving long enough after I pushed—made it clear he was doing it because he wished, not because I forced him to.

He tossed the blade in his hand. It disappeared into the air. The magic was so neat and tidy that the blade blinked out without a sound, flash of light, or puff of air. It was hard not to gape in wonder at the trick. And he knew it. His mouth quirked briefly. "You will stay."

"I beg your pardon?" I glared at him. "I am going to take this and leave."

"You will find that impossible." He turned his back on me, clearly not caring in the least that I was still armed. Prowling over to the large desk before the great windows opposite the door I had entered, he started flipping through papers. "What is your name?"

"I don't see how that has anything to do with the matter." I knew about the tricks the elves and other fae played once they knew a person's name. There was no way he was getting mine.

"Family name then, paranoid one."

"Soleil," I reluctantly offered.

"Ah, I thought so." He straightened, a strange pen glowing in his hand. "You have a brother."

"Yes."

"He is in my service."

"He contracted himself into Whispier's service." I emphasized the name. Why would I deal with an underling when it was Whispier I wished to hurt for taking Solon from me? "I don't know who you are."

This time his eyes lightened. "Do you want to free him?"

I pressed my lips together to suppress the urge to scream at him. I glared at him instead. "Why do you ask?"

"That is a yes then." He plucked a document from the air. The glowing edges gleamed despite the dimness of the room. "What if I offer you a bargain? Your brother's freedom for your companionship."

"What?"

"Friendship, conversation, company—nothing untoward or physical beyond being in the same room frequently."

"Only Whispier has that power," I pointed out.

He tilted his head slightly to the side. "I am Whispier. The fact you haven't figured that out yet doesn't speak well of your intelligence."

"In that case, I might kill you."

His mouth did the funny little quirk again. "You might find me hard to kill."

I eyed him from beneath raised eyebrows. "Is that a challenge?"

"You won't be able to kill me. The bond will prevent you from attacking my person."

"What about maiming? Poisoning? Papercuts?"

His eyes turned silvery. "Papercuts aren't lethal."

I just grinned at him.

"Besides, I heal quickly."

"How about cuts from iron-edged paper?"

"That is a myth, you know." He turned his attention to the glowing edged document. "Iron only gives us a stomachache."

I snorted. "Maybe I will just make it so you wish to die."

A soft sigh of air whispered through the room, and suddenly there was a third presence. The shadow elf from earlier materialized next to Whispier. What had Whispier called him—Casimir? He no longer appeared to be a solid black shadow. Like Whispier, he was tall, lean, and dangerous. Unlike the spymaster, his skin was a dusky brown. His pale green eyes, almost precisely the same shade as Whispier's, flicked from side to side, assessing the two of us.

"Are you quite finished?" he asked the spymaster.

"Almost." With a flick of his slender fingers, Whispier flipped the document to face me. "Our agreement. Your friendship in exchange for your brother's freedom from my service. Your every need will be provided for—food, clothing, housing—in exchange, you will attend me here in my study or other public rooms in the palace."

"And do what?" I demanded. It sounded too good to be true.

He shrugged. "Talk, eat, ignore me, whatever you wish."

"Annoy you?"

He waved the paper impatiently. "Should you wish. Do we have a deal?"

"And Solon is free?"

"The moment you sign this." He offered the glowing pen.

"What about my current master? It isn't as though I am a free woman."

"What is your master's name?"

"Grimore."

His eyes flared silver and he tilted his head to the side. "Interesting. And the nature of your contract is?"

"Thievery in exchange for room, board, and protection."

"Protection from what?" His impassive features tightened. "Do you have a price on your head?"

"Not that I know of. He keeps me safe from those who would prey on a lone woman."

"I can provide that."

I snorted softly. "And who will protect me from you?"

"The agreement will. I bound it into the clauses that I cannot touch you with the intent to hurt or take advantage. The spell will hold me to it."

I had heard of spells reading the intents of a person's actions so that made sense. Food, shelter, protection, and all I had to do in exchange was keep a man company. It sounded almost too good to be true. But then—

I took the paper and read the terms. Solon would be free. I signed the document in glimmering silver ink that appeared to absorb into the paper as I wrote. With the last stroke of my name, I felt the bond take hold with a tingling jolt of magic. The paper disappeared as abruptly as it appeared. Whispier muttered something in Elvish. The shadow elf rolled his eyes and disappeared in a soundless rush of displaced air.

What had I done?

Two

Illeron

"Happy?" I asked my brother as I bent over the morning reports.

Casimir eyed me across the table in the center of my study. "You have to be jesting."

My new companion hadn't arrived yet, but her movements since waking had been reported to me. She had slept fitfully, awakened early, and ate well. Not that any of that mattered. The critical fact was that she was here, and she had promised to stay. Casimir would get off my back about being an ornery hermit.

My brother crossed his arms over his chest. "You cannot coerce friendship. I said you need a friend, a distraction, not that you should manipulate someone into forced companionship."

"I didn't manipulate her."

"No," Casimir grimaced. "You verbally spun her in circles, attempted to influence her with magic—"

"Which failed," I pointed out with perverse pleasure. It made the winning of her company all the sweeter, I realized.

"—and then dangled what you hoped would tempt her into an impulsive decision."

"I knew it was what she wanted." She had been petitioning for her brother's release for years. I had denied them all. It wasn't as though I didn't compensate the man sufficiently for his service. And we were fighting for a good cause.

"How?" Casimir asked but then abruptly straightened. "She is coming."

I didn't need to be warned. I could sense her approach. "I know."

He scanned the room. "Where is she going to sit?"

I shrugged. "Wherever she pleases." I spread the map across the center of the table and dug out the most recent intel report. "Magus Diabolos' minions have been seen as far north as Warlord Kaelen's land just as I warned."

"Good morning," my brother said.

I looked up in time to see him incline his head stiffly toward my companion. Irritation flared through me. Now Casimir would be charm itself.

"How was your first night?" Casimir practically drooled over her.

"Please!" I glared at him. "You know how she did. She barely slept. Don't play innocent."

Casimir glared at me. "Your orders, brother?" The sharp tone in the last word erased any impression of affection between us.

"Go speak with Kaelen and warn him."

Casimir bowed to me perfunctorily and disappeared in a loud crack of violently removed air.

"Now he will sulk for days." I groaned and turned back to my work.

Silence.

She didn't speak. She didn't move. Yet, my senses were preoccupied with the fact that she was there, and she breathed.

Then, she moved.

"How do I know my brother is free? When can I see him?" She walked to the windows overlooking the gardens.

"When our bond sealed, your brother's broke. I honor my promises."

I sorted through missives and reports before checking the map. Far too many mentions of rumors. I needed facts. Reaching for my magic, I summoned another shadow elf. Tyron, a dark-skinned warrior materialized next to me. "Go to—" I hesitated. I had an interloper that I couldn't trust. "Go there." I pointed to the southern border of the woodwose's holdings. "Find the magus stirring up trouble there and report."

"Understood." Tyron blinked and disappeared.

I summoned another. "Go here." He left.

A third appeared. "Bring me Goring," I instructed.

This one hesitated.

"What?" I demanded.

Blagden, one of the most ruthless and efficient elves in my service, was the dark shadow looming next to me. Unlike the others, he had not changed from his shadow form. A blank silhouette of darkness without feature or highlight to add depth, he still managed to make me feel his glare of suspicion. "There is a human in here."

"I am aware."

"A female."

"I don't see how that is any business of yours." My magic rose with a flare of lethal sharpness. My irritation added extra power to my demonstration of power. I didn't threaten him, but I made my position clear.

He transported into the shade of the tree in the conservatory and then through the unspelled door. The spell I maintained on the grounds allowed me to know his every movement.

Blessed silence descended. Well, it would have been blessed except for the fact that she was there—and breathing.

"What did you do with my dagger?" I asked without lifting my gaze from the reports on the table. I needed more intel about what the gargoyles were doing. News from their borders had been too limited.

"Why do some of the shadow elves walk silently and others do not?"

I frowned at the map. "Do I need to have your bedroom searched?"

"Does the difference have to do with their skill level? That one from last night, Casimir, he made a lot of noise when he left."

"That was because he was disgruntled with me." I turned to face her. "I want my dagger back."

She stood against the wall, next to the windows, the only wall that didn't have a piece of furniture shoved up against it. Gone was the brownie-charmed cloak from the previous night. A thick braid of dark auburn hair fell over her slender shoulder. Her sun-kissed features betrayed that she didn't always lurk in the darkness. Intelligence enlivened her features, brightening her eyes and making an otherwise unnoteworthy face arresting.

Her lithe form tensed slightly under my scrutiny, but she didn't retreat. If anything, her response was preparation for a fight. Her dark eyes, a steady brown, studied my features with an unnerving focus. Had they done that last night from the depths of her hood and mask? I wished now that I had demanded she remove her hood then.

"How do I know it is yours?" she demanded.

"I don't steal." I extended my hand toward her in a clear request.

"You do. You stole my brother."

I glared at her. "Your brother volunteered. He signed a standard contract of service in exchange for compensation. I held up my end of the bargain, and he held up his. Give me my dagger."

She didn't even flinch. "The dagger is a plaything, ineffectual as a weapon and by all appearances generally useless. Hardly an object worth all this fuss. What is the dagger to you?"

"Better to ask what its value is to the man who sent you to steal it." I glared at her and flicked my fingers in a clear order for her to hand it over.

Her unnerving eyes narrowed beneath her lowered brows. "Grimore's attachment is equally as puzzling. He would find it disdainful to claim such a farce of a weapon."

I snorted. "It was once his most prized possession. Give me my dagger before I am forced to take it from you."

"You would dare break your word?"

"What are you talking about?" I demanded. My irritation burned at the back of my throat. No one challenged me. Well, no one but Casimir.

"Our agreement, it prevents me from attacking you. That means it also prevents you from attacking me." She smiled smugly. "You aren't the only one who gathers intel."

She was right. Elven agreements needed balance to be binding. Upsetting the balance could nullify the contract. However, there was far more leeway than she supposed. I eyed her person. "Where did you hide it?" I demanded. "It isn't in your room, or you wouldn't be so confident a search there would be fruitless. Your cloak from last night had no pocket charm on it." There was no place for concealment on her person, or at least not room enough for the dagger I sought. That meant she had concealed the dagger somewhere in the house.

I whirled on my heel. "Stay," I ordered before stalking out onto the landing. Crafting a seek-and-find spell, I released it in the direction of the room in which she had slept.

"I will tell you where to find it—"

I turned to find her standing in the doorway of my study.

"I told you to stay."

"I am still inside the room." She gestured to the doorsill, inches from her toes. "Or did you mean for me to freeze in place until your return?" She raised her eyebrows and composed her features into a perfectly innocent mask.

I growled in frustration. The seek-and-find spell returned, whispering its negative results. That left only one alternative. I shoved my way past her, reentering my private domain.

"As I was saying, I will tell you where the dagger is if you tell me why it is so important to you."

As she spoke, I mentally checked off the places she had touched within the room. My gaze fell on the curtains. Pale blue brocade, they were heavy enough to darken the room to almost night at noon. Spelled against fading and dust, they were otherwise innocuous. I glared at them, they were hanging oddly. She had touched them.

Striding across the room, I grabbed the cloth panel that hung closest to where she had lingered at the window. Sliding my hands down the seams, I sought any imperfections. My right hand encountered a lump. She had unpicked, no, sliced the threads holding down the unfinished edge of the fabric and slipped the dagger sheath first into the gap. I pulled it forth.

"I still want to know."

I ignored her. Reaching for my magic, I violently pulled on my storage spell. The dagger disappeared with a savage snap. I stalked over to the map and summoned Dargan.

"Visit Osmond," I ordered with barely contained anger.

Dargan left without a word.

Folding up the maps and stacking the reports, I carried them to my desk. The woman wisely stayed out of my way, retreating to the wall again. Opening the drawer, I tapped the filing spell on it and shoved the stack into the folded space within. Then, not bothering to glance her way, I strode from the room.

To my great annoyance, she followed at a loping pace.

I would do my morning training. Surely that would discourage her from interfering with my routine. The added benefit of using acute focus to keep track of the complicated moves of my opponent would distract me from the fact that she was there. Why were my senses so preoccupied with her breathing?

My usual sparring partner, Maury, waited for me in the middle of the training room at the far end of the palace. His pale skin and ice blond hair set off his cold blue eyes, but none of it was as intimidating as his stature and breadth. I kept more fit than most light elves due to the nature of my work. Still, Maury relished in physical exertion of any kind, which showed in his heavily muscled body.

"Who is she?" he asked as I approached across the subtly matted floor.

"My new pet. Ignore her."

Maury blinked and nodded. "Sparring with or without magic?"

"Without." I was in the mood for physical training more than mental.

"Prepare."

I ran through my stretches before Maury interrupted with an aggressive run at my back. I evaded him, spun, and lunged for the row of clubs hanging on the interior wall. Maury almost beat me there, but I managed to grasp two smooth clubs before he moved in for his next attack.

Avril

Whispier's movements were like music, fluid, beautiful, and powerful. His opponent was less graceful but no less deadly. The pair moved back and forth across the massive space with a series of sharp cracks as their weapons met again and again as they danced.

Thrice the size of the entrance hall, the high walls of the expansive room boasted floor-to-ceiling windows that sent long patterns of light across the floor. At the base of the windows, an array of potted trees, bushes, and plants clustered close to the walls as though for protection from the violence in the center.

I snorted to myself. I didn't know what it was about elves and green things, but the whole palace was peppered with potted plants. Lilies in the corridor, ferns in the bed chambers, and cacti in the kitchen, I was running into displaced plants everywhere I turned.

I glanced at the pair of combatants again. They appeared uninclined to pause any time soon.

To stave off my boredom, I leisurely wandered along the only windowless wall in the room. Clubs, ropes, weights, and other equipment hung along the perimeter. I picked up a selection of balls from a bin. Small enough to fit in the palm of my hand, they felt of equal weight. Giving one of them a tentative toss, I launched it into the air in a controlled arc. Perfect. I grinned in delight. Picking a bit of wall between a stack of towels and a wooden bench, I settled on the floor and crossed my legs.

Launching the first ball into the air, I took great pleasure in the graceful arch. The second followed it. Soon I had five balls whirling through the air, seeming to move like magic from one hand to the other in a dancing arch of colors.

The rhythmic strikes of the smooth round spheres in my hands soothed my frayed nerves. And once my hands fell into a pattern, I could almost convince my mind to calm.

"What are you doing?" Whispier demanded.

I lost my rhythm and faltered in the pattern. Balls scattered in all directions. Despite my efforts, I only managed to catch three. The yellow one bounced twice and then rolled toward the far wall. The remaining one, a bright green, rolled directly over to bump into the spymaster's bare foot.

When had he removed his shoes? For some reason, I couldn't reconcile naked toes with the vicious spymaster I knew him to be.

"Juggling." I lifted my chin defiantly. If he was going to ignore me, I intended to entertain myself. "Surely you have heard of it. It is a human trick of hurling objects through the air without magic."

He picked up the wayward ball and studied it.

"Are we finished?" The huge blond elf asked. A flicker of uncertainty passed across his face as he glanced from me to Whispier and back.

Whispier dismissed the elf with a wave of his hand. "Tomorrow."

The man nodded and left.

"An intriguing choice of occupation."

I snorted. "Not that you offered me much alternative."

He tossed the ball into the bin that it had come from and reached over my head for a towel.

"So, elves do sweat when they exert themselves," I observed without moving. "I always wondered."

He stilled with the towel to his face. Then, slowly he lowered it to eye me. "What did you think we did?"

I shrugged. "Not sweat. It seems so base for such an elevated species."

For a moment, his face froze. Then, he abruptly turned away.

Without really thinking through the consequences, I threw the red ball at his retreating back. It bounced harmlessly off his left shoulder.

He came to a halt but didn't turn.

I threw the second ball, this one blue. It struck the middle of his back.

He let his head fall back, and he glanced at the ceiling as though pleading for patience from a higher power.

Determined to get more of a reaction, I whipped the last ball at his head, a purple one.

He moved quicker than I could flinch and caught the ball right before it hit his head. Irritation sparked in his eyes. One moment he was about a dozen feet away; the next, he was standing over me, fist tightening around the ball so that his knuckles whitened.

"What are you doing?" he demanded.

I slapped a grin on my face, despite my sudden fear at the anger darkening his eye color. "Testing the bond to see if it can detect intent."

He closed his eyes, straightened, and took a long, careful breath. "It can. And apparently, the intent to irritate doesn't trigger it. Are you satisfied?"

I shrugged. "For now."

He groaned. "I am going to go wash up and then do some research in the library. You may meet me there. Do you need a guide, or did you memorize the location when planning your mission to invade my home?"

"I know where it is." No point in playing sly since we both knew I had researched my mission. I bounced to my feet with purposeful enthusiasm. "I will fetch the rest of the balls." I strode off to retrieve the errant balls from among the potted crowd. After years of risking life and limb stealing for my master, antagonizing an elf was turning out to be far less perilous than expected.

As much as I didn't appreciate the result of Whispier interrupting my heist, I could do some good while I was caught. The elf spymaster was far too crotchety. He needed some loosening up.

THREE

Illeron

My time in the library was my favorite part of the day. Even when I couldn’t find time to read any of the tomes surrounding me, I loved to be near them. Centuries of elven knowledge, cultural treasures from all our continent's species, and literary works in multiple languages filled my shelves. Now, if only my new companion could restrain herself long enough for me to actually work, all would be well.

To my shock, I found her curled up in my favorite chair with a book on the history of the elves. Glancing up, she noted my appearance with a nod and then returned to reading.

I stood there for a moment in wonder. Maybe she wasn’t a complete hoyden.

I considered the costs and benefits of expelling her from my favorite chair and concluded that leaving her alone would probably bring me the most peace. I sat on the other side of the table from my usual position and accessed my magical filing system. I had just arranged my notes when my first spy arrived. With a soundless puff, he appeared next to my favorite chair.

The shadow elf blinked down at my new companion.

"She is my new pet. Ignore her."

Avril looked up from her book and smiled up at the elf before returning to reading.

My spy made his report and left. So, it followed for three hours. Then the last spy arrived, his entrance just as innocuous as all the others.

Unlike every other one of my men, Lynan glared at my new companion. When I called her my pet, his lips twisted.

For her part, she didn't respond. A quick glance at the elf's face, and she resumed reading.

However, when Lynan began his report, she became fidgety. She dropped her book at one point bringing his words to a complete halt as we both watched her practically dive out of the chair to pick it up from the floor.

"Sorry, I slipped," she apologized.

"Anyway," Lynan concluded. "There is little to report on the northern border beyond the usual skirmishes between the most restless warlords and the woodwose."

I nodded curtly and finished my last note.

"That is all."

He bowed his head to me and then disappeared as silently as he came.

"He lies." Avril hissed into the displaced air.

I frowned over at her. "Best wait until he leaves my property before voicing such accusations."

"Fine." She set the book on the edge of the table. "Is he gone now?"

I traced his path from my presence until it reached the edge of my domain. Then, I nodded.

She leaned forward, intently serious. "Batair and Cathral have been itching for a fight with the woodwose for three months. However, they haven't managed to stock up enough provisions between them to risk all-out war. When they have their provisions, their joint forces will unsettle the balance in the region and possibly lead to the complete subjugation of the woodwose."

Intrigued by her sudden animation, I considered the possibility. It might be worth investigating. Fortunately, I had already sent Tyron to gather intel near the disputed border.

"Why mention it?" I began clearing away my work, sorting, stacking, and then filing the notes.

"I detest liars and your elf spy is clearly lying to you." She watched the process with intent focus. "Aren't you going to do anything?"

I tilted my head to one side. "Why should I believe the word of a woman not willing to trust me with her name?"

"I don't lie."

"Neither do I, yet you clearly don't trust me."

"I have heard stories about what elves do to humans when they acquire the knowledge of their true name." She shivered.

"Worse than binding them to companionship?"

Fear flickered in the depths of her brown eyes. She shivered again. "Much worse."

My curiosity was piqued. Which of the horror tales spread about my species over the years had caused that revulsion?

"You clearly have good reason to abstain from speaking your name to me." I rose to my feet. "But it is too late."

Her eyes widened in surprise.

"I already have it."

"How?"

"Your brother named you as next of kin on his contract." I picked up her discarded book from the edge of the table. "I have had it all along, yet I didn't use it." Arching an eyebrow at her, I passed by her to reshelve the tome.

She stood and followed me, practically on my heels. "Then why didn't you use it to get me to give you the dagger?"

I halted abruptly, turning to face her.

She stumbled so that we almost ended up standing nose to nose, with me looking directly down into her widened eyes.

Leaning close so that my breath brushed her face, I quietly stated, "No moral being would take a person's will from them."

She quirked her head to the side, studying my expression. "And you consider yourself a moral being?"

"I do." I turned away and slid the tome into place. "Do you want food?"

"Yes, please." Her sudden and effusively genuine grin hit me in the gut. Oh, to be so uninhibited...

We left the library and headed toward the kitchen down on the first floor.

My household manager and childhood friend, Ergon, awaited us just outside the dining room door.

"Pardon, Master Whispier, but the dining room is still being cleaned."

I glared at him. Typically, Ergon kept the household running like a well-oiled machine, all the parts silently working in the background and out of sight and mind.

"Voles," he mouthed to me.

I groaned.

"Voles?" Avril asked.

"They ate through the roots of the table, making it unstable, and the chandeliers are shedding their leaves." Ergon's gaze flicked from me to Avril and back. "Would you prefer to eat in the study or the library perhaps?"

"The study," I declared. "I am not sure if my new pet is housebroken yet."

Avril snorted softly.

"Very well." Ergon flashed Avril a smile before bowing and gliding off in the direction of the kitchen.

I frowned after him. When had I last seen Ergon smile? He wasn't exactly an effusive personality.

When I returned to my study with Avril on my heels, I was annoyed to find Ergon had already anticipated my choice. Two place settings were spread on either side of one of the table's corners. I efficiently moved one setting around to the opposite side of the table, so the whole width lay between us.

"I don't bite." Avril claimed the chair opposite the door. She bounced into the chair and flung her slender legs over one chair arm. "Despite your accusations."

Too restless to sit, I began pacing the length of the table opposite her. My mind turned over the details of the morning reports. The fact that unrest continued to spread among the warlords was disquieting alone. However, the possibility that the warlords could be joining forces against the woodwose, an un-antagonistic warrior species, added extra concern. If it was true, I needed to know why. What was motivating them? Were they acting of their own volition or under the influence of a rogue magus? My stomach soured.

"What are you doing?"

"Thinking." I mentally reviewed the list of known magus lamias. None had been reported in the area recently, and all had been accounted for within the last month.

"With your feet?"

I snorted softly. "Movement calms my brain and helps me focus."

"So, when you were exercising—"

"Drilling," I interjected.

"…drilling earlier, you were thinking?"

"No. Then, I was just drilling."

Ergon entered. Four silently moving servants followed in his wake. I purposefully kept pacing, but Avril straightened in her seat, moving her feet off the arm of the chair and slipping them under the table.

"We took into consideration some of your suggestions." Ergon bowed politely over Avril, who gazed up at him. "I hope you find our lunch selections more to your taste."

"I am sure it will be delicious," she assured him with a friendly smile. "Breakfast was delicious."

"You are too kind. Your expression said otherwise."

"I just didn't expect such strong seasoning."

"Not everyone shares Master Whispier's tastes." Ergon didn't even have the presence of mind to look uncomfortable expressing a less than flattering opinion of my preferences. In fact, he smiled graciously down at my companion.

"If you objected, you should've said something," I snapped.

"We have no objections, Master Whispier. Our food is prepared separately." He turned and bowed to me with his customary reserve. "Your meal was prepared as you prefer."

Ergon and the others retreated, and suddenly Avril and I were alone again. "What is wrong with the way I season my food?"

"Nothing." She shrugged. "If you wish to sear your tastebuds to numbness, it is your own prerogative. I prefer more subtle seasoning."

She picked up her fork and loaded it with a bite. Then, after appearing to taste it with her complete attention, she smiled. "Delicious. I will have to let Ergon and the cook know." Loading another forkful, she glanced up at me. "If you are finished thinking, I recommend eating. Aren't some of your underlings due to return with their reports this afternoon?"

"They are." I pulled out my chair and sat. "And I am fully capable of eating and thinking at the same time."

"I never thought you weren't." She blinked at me innocently, but I was not deceived.

We ate in silence for a few moments.

"Are you always this disgruntled?" She suddenly asked.

"No." I stabbed a bite of meat.

We ate in silence for a few minutes. Then a soft plunk of something small striking the table next to my plate brought my attention into sharp focus. My fork stilled.

With a delicate ping, a pea bounced off my water glass and landed in the cheese sauce, coating my broccoli. I lifted my head.

Avril hastily picked up her fork, but not before I saw her wipe her fingers on the linen napkin in her lap.

My eyebrows lifted. "Testing the bond?"

"Naturally." She shoveled a bite into her mouth and chewed with apparent innocence.

I set down my utensils. "Peas are hardly weapons."

"Unless they are poisoned." A gleam of something playful flickered in her dark eyes, but no further trace of amusement made it through her expression.

"I doubt they are poisoned. My cook has been employed by me for decades. If he meant me harm, I suspect he would have made more of a move before now than poisoned peas."

"Maybe he suddenly has a motive."

I closed my eyes. "What possible motive would he have to harm me?"

She opened her mouth, but a soft thump of someone landing heavily on the floor behind me interrupted. I reached for my magic. The spell for summoning my weapon tingled my fingertips before I rose and turned to face the new arrivals.

"Whew!" A massive man with slightly gray-tinged skin stood in the center of my study. His eyes were wide as his massive shoulders heaved with a series of heavy breaths. "That never gets easier."

Next to him stood Adham, one of my most trusted shadow elves. Wry amusement sparkled in his pale eyes as his shadow form melted away, and his features became clear again. "You are the only one who reacts this way to wraithwalking."

"Troy!" I neutralized my spell. "It is a pleasure to see you again."

The gargoyle stood a handful of inches taller than me, but his heavily muscled frame dwarfed mine in volume. It made sense considering the wings he had stowed invisibly against his back. Flying with them required a tremendous amount of strength and endurance. To a one, the gargoyle species were broad-chested and large-shouldered men and women even in their human forms.

Troy, a prince of the western eyrie, had been my friend since we were both young. I held out my arms, and he met me halfway, crushing me to his chest in a massive hug. He would have lifted my feet from the ground, too, if I hadn't planted them on the rug with my magic.

"Arg! You grow heavy in your old age, Illeron." He released me, stepping back to pound my back with one massive hand. "You are overdue for a visit to our eyrie. Avia asks after you often. A pledgekeeper should see his charge at least once a year, and it has been three since your last coming."

"The world is a restless place." I motioned for Troy to join us. "Would you like food? Wine? Tea?"

"None for me." Troy walked toward the table only to pause and tilt his head to one side. "And who is this?"

Avril had stood to her feet. Her hand resting a bit too casually on her hip. I suspected she concealed a weapon there.

"My companion, Avril." I nodded to Troy. "Don't worry, pet. Troy doesn't bite. Well, not unless you are wrestling with him."

"I never. Not since I was a fledgling."

"Sit." I reclaimed my chair. Troy accepted my invitation, drawing out the chair at the place at the end of the table. Avril hesitantly reclaimed her spot. Despite her efforts to appear at ease, she deceived no one. Avril was far too tense. Troy met my gaze with raised eyebrows when she studied her plate for a moment.

I shrugged. Perhaps she had issues with gargoyles. Now wasn't the time to figure it out.

"The name is Troy." He offered an open palm to her in the traditional greeting of the gargoyles.

She very reluctantly touched fingertips with him as required. Then, she immediately retracted her fingers.

"Why so skittish?" Troy asked. "I don't harm the unarmed."

"Ah, but she is armed," I pointed out.

Troy's gaze took in Avril's quickly dropped hand from her waist with amusement. "So she is. As a rule, I don't carry off friends of friends."

"Avia would object," I added for Avril's benefit.

Troy laughed.

"And who is Avia?" Her brown eyes darted from Troy to me and back.

"My wife," Troy responded. "I was just kidding about the flying off with people. I never carry anyone off against their will, except confirmed villains, of course."

"Such as?" Curiosity brightened her eyes as they studied the giant gargoyle next to her.

"Those in the service of a magus or someone invading the eyrie." He considered her with a playful grin. "Planning an invasion?"

"Only a fool would even contemplate it." I filled my fork. "Any of that kind of activity along your borders recently?"

Troy turned the full force of his personality upon me. With a grimace, he admitted there had been. "We haven't had this much activity along our borders for forty years. Few of the trespassers are actually interested in our treasures, though. They are trying to steal our children, which is much worse." Then he turned back to Avril. "Which brings me back to my question. Why are you so skittish around gargoyles?"

"It could just be you," I suggested.

Undeterred, Troy didn't turn away from studying my companion, who avoided meeting his eyes.

"I was stalked by a gargoyle a few months back." She shoved food around her plate with an empty fork. "He snatched me and then threatened to drop me from a great height if I didn't give him the information he wanted."

"Did you comply?"

"No." Her gaze flicked up to assess his expression. "I didn't have the information he thought I did."

"Did he release you?"

"No." She drew the word out softly. Her assessment widened to include my features as well. I kept them neutral. "I ripped his wing and ran."

"Obviously to great success," Troy observed.

"Why do you say that?" Her finely arched brow creased above her nose.

"You are alive, aren't you?"

She smiled, a sudden lightening of expression that seemed to brighten the room. "True."

"Let me assure you that not a single gargoyle in my eyrie would dare do that to anyone, or they would be answerable to me. Humans are not playthings to be flung about like rag dolls."

She bowed her head to him graciously. "I appreciate your wise perspective, Rexaer Troy. If only all gargoyles shared your morals."

Troy threw himself back in his chair with a great crow. "Ah, she has fooled me. Playing the timid child and then calling me by the title only known among my people. Why the fraud?"

"No deceit, Rexaer. I speak without guile. Just because I am appropriately hesitant thanks to my experience, I am not one to embark on a mission without gathering all the intel I can about those I might meet."

"So, you purposefully crossed into gargoyle territory?" Troy's narrowed gaze held no anger, but there was no way for my companion to know that.

Silently, I rested my fork on the edge of my plate and watched the interplay between them with interest.

"I knew my mark might purposefully cross into your people's territory in hopes that I would give up my pursuit."

"And the gamble didn't work?"

She nudged her broccoli. "It did, sadly. I did not count on him being allied with a gargoyle."

"Was this mark in the service of a magus?"

"Yes." She frowned. "My master, Warlord Grimore, does all he can to oppose the magus plague."

"Grimore, you say?" Troy's gaze slid over to me. "I thought you called her companion."

"She is."

She tensed at Troy's tone. "I misspoke. Grimore is my former master. Master Whispier is now my master."

"Companion," I corrected. She lifted her face and met my gaze across the table. "You are my companion, and I am yours. We are equals in this bond."

The depths of her dark eyes flashed with sudden, intense emotion. Troy moved to speak, but I lifted my hand to stop him. "You wish to say something, Avril?"

"There is nothing equal about our bond. I agreed to spend time in your presence. What have I received in return?"

"Safety, security, food, rest—"

"And no freedom."

"Hardly. You can come and go as you please. Just return by nightfall." I purposefully picked up my glass with a careful movement. "I told you that you were free to do anything short of attacking me."

A biscuit bounced off my head with such force that it rebounded across the room and struck the far wall.

Troy burst into booming laughter.

By the time I lowered my cup, Avril's attention was once again fixed on her plate.

FOUR

Avril

"Why do they target the fledglings?" I asked.

A week had passed since Troy the gargoyle's visit. During that time, I had been trying to reconcile the fact that the rough and tumble gargoyle was close friends with the aloof and reserved elf across the table from me. The afternoon light filtered through the library windows. Tracing patterns across the tabletop, it played with the red highlights in the dark brown curls rioting over his forehead. He leaned over the documents on the table before him.

In a surprisingly rare moment of stillness, his hands bracketed the edges of a map. Only the quick movements of his closed eyes and the sharp relief of the tendons standing out on the backs of his elegant hands betrayed his intensity, well, that and the standoffish air about him.

I picked up my eraser. It was a small blob of rubber that Ergon had provided when I asked for writing supplies days ago.

I rubbed my fingertips over the smooth surface.

It wasn't like it was a pencil. If it hit him, it wouldn't hurt–much.

I chucked the rubber blob at his head. It bounced off his temple and hit the table with an explosion of tingling elf magic. A mist of green encased the eraser and whipped it at my head. I caught it. For a brief moment, the mist fought my hold before dissipating into nothingness.

"Must you?" he asked without looking up.

"You were ignoring me." I shifted in my chair, which I had recently learned was his favorite in the library. "I was trying to get your attention."

"I am always aware of you." A subtle note of irritation tinged his voice. "Much to my annoyance." Suddenly straightening, he pinned me with a deadly sharp glare. "What do you want?"

"Why do the invaders into Troy's eyrie target the fledglings?" I asked, ignoring the strange flutter in my gut that had nothing to do with fear. I liked it when he was intently focused on me, even if it manifested in a glare.

"Easier to subdue." He arched his brows at me. "Can you see anyone willingly attempting to bring Troy to heel?"

"No." The gargoyle would tear them to pieces first.

"Besides that, the young are easier to bind in a way that prevents them from breaking away later when they are full grown."

"But why keep them?"

He studied my face. "Magus lamias capture naturally magical species for only one thing: draining. They capture their victims, bind them so they cannot access their magic, and siphon off the victim's magic. Imagine someone scraping your soul from your body one razor-thin layer at a time. It causes excruciating agony."

A wave of horror followed by nausea passed over me.

"You didn't know?" he asked.

I shook my head.

"Grimore had never let me go on a raid on a magus' stronghold. He only assigned me to scouting missions." I shivered. "How do we stop them, these magic vampyres?"

"That is easier said than done."

"What has been done already?" I asked, rolling the eraser between my fingers. "Are they centralized? What are their defenses?" I leaned forward in my eagerness. "What about their weaknesses? They must have weaknesses."

Something in his extraordinary eyes shifted, and the color warmed to be greener and less silver. "They do."

"They do what?" I demanded.

"They do have weaknesses and defenses. No, they are not centralized, which is the biggest part of our problems of late. They are multiplying out of nowhere, and we can't figure out how."

"And what has been done?"

"It would be simpler to specify what we have not done. We have been fighting this war for centuries, and we are losing." Grief slipped through his mask, pulling at his fine mouth and causing him to close his eyes as though to block out the emotional impact of the war. "They have only just begun targeting gargoyles, which means they are growing bolder."

"And elves?"

He shook his head. "We have been spared so far, but the brownies, woodwose, and other weaker species with natural magic have been targeted since the beginning. At first, it was individuals, the outliers of the population. But for the past two decades, families have disappeared." He grimaced as he considered the empty tabletop between us. "Consider yourself lucky you have not known such loss."

But I had. Well, at least to a smaller degree, I had. Whispier had leaked the information that led to my parents' death and then taken my brother from me, the two events that had left me desperate and alone. Because of those losses, I had been desperate, turning to Warlord Grimore and his offer of training in exchange for shelter and protection. At least, Solon still lived and was now free.

Whispier was already refocused on his work. Hands splayed, head bent, and shoulders hunched in concentration, he didn't respond. I didn't bother to attempt gaining his attention again and perused the shelves in search of distraction from the memories crowding my head.

I picked up the book on elven history I had spotted the day before and hid behind it. This time I didn't make a show of reading. I mulled over how I could've missed something so significant going on around me. True, magus lamias were a blight on the land, causing trouble for the warlords, harassing the kings in the north and south. But I hadn't heard of them draining fae creatures of their magic.

Illeron

"The unrest among the Unseelie is growing. They are demanding the right to rampage over the fields of the human farms bordering their land." Casimir stood in the middle of the library as he gave his report.

Two weeks had passed since Avril had arrived. She lounged in my favorite spot with her legs flung over one arm of the chair.

"What do you think?" I asked her, interrupting Casimir mid-recitation.

My brother halted mid word, but my companion didn't even lift her head.

"Avril?"

"Hmm…?" She blinked her dark brown eyes as she regarded me almost sleepily.

"Are we boring you?" I asked.

"No, but this book is." She shut it with a snap and slid it onto the table. "What was your first question?"

Casimir's irritation manifested on the edges of my senses. As his shadow magic flared, the shadows grew opaquer, and a few whips of darkness crept across the floor.

Arvil spotted one as it emerged from a shadow and began a meandering journey toward my brother's feet. She straightened and leaned to the side to keep it in sight.

"I was wondering what your opinion was regarding the Unseelie's demands that they have a right to rampage across the human farms near their borders." I watched with amusement as she suddenly perched on seat of the chair as the black whisp of shadow magic reached Casimir's foot and melted into him.

"Did that become part of you, or did you call it to you?" She asked Casimir as she unfolded from her chair and stalked around the table to study the floor between the shadow and Casimir.

My brother glared at her. "It is a manifestation of my magic."

"He is annoyed." I explained. "Whisps of darkness are attracted to him when he emotes strongly."

"I am not emoting," Casimir responded.

At the same moment, Avril asked, "Why?"

My brother's frown deepened as he sighed softly. "Illeron, why are you delaying my report?"

"I am asking her opinion," I pointed out.

"Whatever for?"

"She is human."

"And that gives her a right to comment on everything to do with humans?" His dark brows rose dramatically. "It isn't as though she has a vested interest in all humanity."

"I thought she might have an opinion I should consider before I act."

Casimir groaned. "I should've never—" Then he bit off his statement.

I smirked at him. As much as I was enjoying my new companion, the fact that I could use her to annoy Casimir, entertained me nearly as much. "It was your suggestion."

"A fact I am painfully aware of," he retorted.

"Are you two finished?" Avril asked abruptly.

We both turned our heads to regard her. Laughter danced in her eyes, causing her features to brighten. I found myself enthralled.

"I have a question," she declared.

"Yes?"

"Who owns the land?"

Casimir answered first. "That is debatable."

"The Unseelie claim that it is within their agreed upon borders negotiated back when we all first came to settle among humans," I explained.

"And the humans claim that the Unseelie modified the agreement without their consent, thereby making the claim invalid," Casimir added.

She considered this for a moment. "Is there record of the original agreement in anyone's possession aside from the Unseelies'?"

Casimir tilted his head ever so slightly to the side. "In fact, there is. It is in the Seelie King's possession."

"Then, perhaps he should be consulted," Avril suggested.

"Which was what I was going to request," I said.

Casimir nodded. "Then, I will send a messenger to inquire of the Seelies." With a slight shifting of air, he left.

Avril frowned at the small whirl of dust skittering across the floor in his wake. "Is he always so abrupt?"

"Frequently." I turned back to my scattered pages on the table. "You will get used to it."

She let out a soft sound that I suspected was to say she doubted it. Then, she returned to her chair and I to my work.

Avril

A soft whump signaled the appearance of one of Master Whispier's shadow elves. I didn't even bother looking up from arranging the stack of book options I had set on the table hours before. I loved having so much time to read, but with such a wide selection to choose from, I frequently struggled to settle my focus on one at a time.

Suddenly, something slammed against the window overlooking the gardens.

Whispier and his elven spy lifted their heads but didn't move to check on the window.

When they returned to their conversation, clearly not intending to investigate the noise, I set aside my book and rose to my feet. When I approached the window, the view looked like it should. Sunlight played over the orderly paths of the garden and the expansive swaths of grass. Then, I scanned the sky. The deep blue expanse offered a clear view for miles. The only blemish in the perfect color was a formation of dark birds flying toward the palace.

Strange. They were unusually large for birds.

"Master Whispier?" I glanced over my shoulder. "You might want to see this."

I turned back to the window only to jump backward. A filthy creature with a woman's head and arms clung to the outer ledge beyond the glass by her huge taloned claws. She turned her maddened red-ringed eyes on me, and she grinned with half-crazed bloodlust. Then lifting a claw, she smashed the window.

I scrambled back from the cascading glass, reaching for my hidden knife.

"Avril, run!" Whispier's urgent voice reached me moments before someone grabbed my arm and yanked me behind them. I only caught an impression of a lean, well-muscled shoulder before the harpy opened her mouth.

A piercing scream ripped the room, rising in volume. I covered my ears, trying to muffle the sound, but to no avail. A sharp shard of agony pierced my head as both of my eardrums burst, plunging me into an eerie world of complete silence and pain. A glimpse of Whispier's rage-filled features as he stabbed the first harpy passed before me as the pain in my head became too much. The contorted face of a shrieking harpy diving claws first at my head was the last thing I saw before darkness claimed my senses.

I woke to movement and the stench of rotting flesh. A throbbing in my temples assured me it wasn't just a dream. Someone held me close. A firm chest beneath my palms, a solid lean arm behind my shoulders, and the unique scent of my new elven master filled my only working senses. Those sensations were almost comforting. Then, it dawned on me. I couldn't see anything, and worse, I couldn't hear anything. Someone was touching my face, and a tingle of magic was working within my head.

Meddling elf! I didn't want him in my head! I shoved at him.

He didn't let go, but I did manage to dislodge his fingers from my face.

"No! Get out of my head!" The vibration of my words worked through my throat and head, but no sound reached my ears. Tears flooded my eyes. I was deaf!

I collapsed against my captor and burst into tears.

Whispier roughly tightened his one-armed grip on my shoulders, trapping me against his chest as his free hand completely covered the right side of my face. The pressure of his fingers against my skin was just short of painful, and his magic suddenly flooded my head in a tingling wave of scents. Grass, moss, and the rustle of the wind through the trees, the smells and the sensations of spring in the forest overwhelmed me as I cried. I couldn't stop him.

Then a pop on the right side of my head.

"...fighting me. I am trying to heal one of her ears," Whispier's voice said from next to me. "Hold still, love. I am almost finished."

I stiffened slightly, pressing against his hand to turn my face upward toward the sound of his voice just as the light returned with a snap.

"The alarms have been reset, Master Whispier. I will go seek out your brother for you."

Whispier's handsome face came into focus inches above my own. Darkened moss green eyes rimmed in silver and threaded with blue studied my features with growing concern.

"Did I hurt you?" he asked huskily.

I shook my head slightly without breaking my gaze from his.

"May I resume healing you?" His breath caressed my face. His voice sounded strange when heard with only one ear.

"Yes." My voice was muffled.

His fingers caressed my temple, lacing into the loosened strands of hair that had escaped my braid. He molded his hand to the shape of my head. The green of his eyes darkened further, and the silver seemed to glow against the darkness. Awareness of his closeness flooded through me. He radiated warmth and a soothing sense of comfort despite the intensity of his gaze. I was half tempted to close my eyes and shut out the discomfort of his gaze, preferably to focus on the sensations of his embrace.

With a soft pop, I could hear fully again. His breathing caught in his chest with a barely noticeable hitch as the tingling in my head stopped. Pain tightened his features for a fraction of a second before he had composed them again. But he couldn't disguise his breathing, shallower, quicker than it should be, and clearly abnormal.

"You are injured," I realized.

"It is nothing." He slowly released me. His hands lingered on my shoulders longer than necessary, even if he was checking to make sure I was steady on my feet. Then, he took a hesitant step backward.

Casimir appeared in Whispier's shadow and elegantly sidestepped to a more socially acceptable distance. "The harpies have been driven off the grounds. We are still investigating how they managed to get as far as the palace wall before being detected." The shadow elf suddenly frowned. "Illeron, you are bleeding."

Whispier grimaced. "I am aware."

"Then heal yourself."

Whispier closed his eyes. "I am working on it." He wavered slightly as the tingling sensation of magic filled the air around him. Casimir reached out and steadied his brother.

I pulled a chair around and pushed it against the back of Whispier's knees. He collapsed into it with a groan.

Blood saturated the back of his shirt, seeping swiftly into the brocade of the chair, staining it green.

"What can I do to help?" I asked, frantic with the thought that he might die. "He shouldn't be bleeding that fast. Should I put pressure on it?"

Casimir grunted. "Usually, he doesn't need anything. If he hadn't foolishly healed someone who clearly could've waited, the bleeding would've stopped already."

"She needed help. You know harpies carry infections deadly to other creatures. Humans are so fragile."

"Still, she wasn't dying yet. You could've healed yourself first." As he chastised his brother, Casimir was swiftly cutting away the back of Whispier's shirt to reveal a series of deep gashes. It appeared one of the harpies had landed on his back, sinking her claws deep into the muscle and bone of his shoulders.

"I healed the bones before I started helping her," Whispier protested.

Despite his argument, I didn't like how pale he was. Grabbing the tablecloth from a nearby table, I folded it into a thick pad and offered it to Casimir.

"What is that for?" he demanded, glaring at the cloth.

"Applying pressure." I grimaced at his blank stare. "To encourage the wound to close up and scab. At the very least, it will stop him from bleeding so quickly. I don't know how much blood elves need, but bleeding too much will kill a human."

"Elves too," Whispier muttered. "Let her."

"Fine. Do what you will. I am going to try and find a healer." He skewered me with a dark glare. "If he dies before I return, rest assured I am going to hunt you down for an accounting of why."

"Understood." I nodded. "Don't let him die, or you will kill me."

Casimir snorted and left in a slight whoosh that stirred the scattered papers on the floor.

"He won't kill you." Whispier leaned over the arm of the chair, offering me a clear view of his wound.

"You didn't see his face." I crossed to him and pressed the cloth pad against the worst bleeding gouge.

Whispier sucked air sharply through his teeth. The muscles of his back tensed beneath my hand.

"I am sorry." As aggravating as he was, I didn't wish him harm. "Your brother isn't happy that you healed me first."

"Not his decision." He groaned. "Never was."

"That won't stop him from killing me if you die."

Whispier's soft chuckle filled the ruined library. "I won't die."

"Is that bravado or truth-speaking? I am not very familiar with elven anatomy, but you have lost a lot of blood." Green speckles and smears were mixed with more typical rust-colored stains on the floor. "Wait, where was I injured?" Feeling my face and head with my free hand, I found it all whole.

"She attempted to rip out your throat, except she missed."

I ran my hand down my throat. There was some tenderness around my left collarbone, but only smooth skin met my fingertips.

"The phantom pain should clear up by nightfall." His voice grew softer. "I think I found all of your injuries, but if I missed one, I can…." He slumped forward.

Abandoning the cloth, I moved just fast enough to stop him from smashing his face as he sprawled out of his chair and to the floor. His continued ominous silence left me scrambling to check for a pulse. I did know elves had hearts and, if they lived, pulses. Thankfully a strong, steady beat met my questing fingers when I finally found his wrist. Retrieving the pad of stained cloth, I reapplied pressure to the back of his shoulder and prayed that he wouldn't die before Casimir returned.

FIVE

Illeron

"You risked too much." Casimir stood over my bed, glaring at me in the darkness of my room. Standing in the shadows cast by the moonlight, my brother was nearly invisible in the dimness. Only the angry glitter of his silvery-green eyes glinted out of the velvet blackness.

I groaned as I rolled on my side away from his judging gaze. I wasn't in the mood for this discussion. My back and shoulders burned where the healer had placed a slow-working healing spell on the gashes. My skin would be whole by midnight and the scars gone before morning, but that thought did little to soothe my discomfort.

"You should've dealt with your own injuries and called the healer for her." He flitted through the shadows, materializing across from me again. Arms folded over his chest. "She wasn't worth the risk of dying."

"I wasn't dying." I glared up at him. "You know we are harder to kill than that." My back spasmed as muscles grew together. I bit back an oath as I rolled onto my stomach and buried my face in my pillow.

"It wasn't as though she was dying," Casimir muttered.

I turned my head so my voice wouldn't be muffled. He had to hear this. "She was. If I hadn't acted, she would've bled out on the floor within minutes. That harpy knew what to target. She ripped Avril's neck open from ear to collarbone." I grimaced as another muscle clenched in my back. Never had my years of studying human anatomy proven so important as in those first few moments after I reached her. The memory of her torn flesh brought a fresh wave of horror. Clinical objectiveness had melted away at the sight of her slender body sprawled on the cold floor with her lifeblood pulsing from her with frightening speed. "If I didn't know better, I would think she was being targeted."

"Why?" Casimir snorted softly. "She is a lowly thief and a bad one at that. I spotted her long before she reached your study. Only an idiot would walk through an unspelled door without realizing it was a trap." He shifted his weight soundlessly. "Besides, you didn't have to heal her to the extent you did. You could've just stabilized her, and that would've satisfied the binding."

"Regardless of what our binding required, humans are fragile. I couldn't risk her sickening or dying."

Shadow wisps of darkness began gathering around Casimir. His voice grew dangerous. "You didn't bond with her," he demanded. "Tell me you didn't."

I blinked up at him in confusion. "Of course not." Bonding was more like marriage. A binding was simply a contract, that was all.

"Just a binding spell."

"Balanced and breakable."

"Good."

I rolled onto my side, propping myself up with one arm. "Why the dramatics?"

He snorted. "You are attached to her."

"I wouldn't go that far." Memories of my panic came to mind, but I brushed them away. I hated seeing any creature in pain, not just her. "We are still far from what you fear. She still hurls things at me regularly."

"Just remember what bonding with a human means. No life-lengthening serum will keep them alive as long as you have left. You would be condemning yourself to a half-life after hers is done." He glanced away. "I am not sure I could stand watching that."

"I have no plans to. Now leave me be. I need rest." I rolled back onto my stomach and pressed my face into my pillow to further emphasize I was done talking.

Casimir left in a silent breeze of air.

I mulled over who, if anyone, might want to target my new companion.

Avril

Exhaustion greeted me the following day. Forcing myself from bed, I dressed and appeared in the kitchen for breakfast at the usual time. A brownie with exceptional culinary skills, the cook set a plate of meat, eggs, fruit, and bread on the counter. He had earlier introduced himself as Waldorf.

"That is the same clothing you wore yesterday," Waldorf observed.

"I have nothing else to wear. It isn't as though I had a chance to pack before moving in." Reaching for the fork, I jabbed the first egg. But before I could pop it into my mouth, Ergon entered the room.

"Lady Avril!" he exclaimed.

"What?" I dropped the fork on the edge of the plate with a clatter.

"Why are you wearing that? There is blood down the front." He surveyed my shirt with horror.

"And across the back as well," Waldorf pointed out.

"As I was saying, this is all I have to wear." I sighed. I was very aware of the mingled rust and green blood stains. The quantity of rust-colored stains on the back of the shirt alone made me suspect blood loss was the cause of my unusual exhaustion.

Ergon nodded. "Makes sense. But that must be rectified, immediately." He waved to indicate I should resume eating. "I will have something for you by the time you finish that."

He disappeared in the direction of the front hall.

I turned back to my food. The first bite was delicious. "If this keeps up, I am going to become a flabby slug," I commented before taking another mouthful.

"What do you mean?" Waldorf asked as he worked a mound of dough.

"I am not sure how elven metabolism works, but humans have to exercise regularly, or we lose our shape. Fat appears around our middles, and we grow weak."

"The same happens to elves." He eyed me. "Perhaps not as quickly."

"Really? I have never heard of a fat elf."

Waldorf chuckled. "Then you haven't met many elves."

"Actually, my first elf was Master Whispier." I shoveled another bite into my mouth.

"You met him before?"

I shook my head. "Nope. My whole experience with elves has been completely contained in the last few weeks."

"Which explains so much." Master Whispier entered through the glass doors that opened into the gardens. "Why haven't you changed?" He surveyed my clothing with steely disapproval.

I sighed. "Is everyone going to comment on my clothing?"

"These should serve for the time being," Ergon announced as he breezed into the room with a pile of folded clothing draped over his arm. "I will see to having some things made for you, but until then, you cannot wear that."

"Why not?" I asked.

At the same time, Master Whispier enquired, "Where exactly did you find those, Ergon?"

"Your chambers."

Strangely, Whispier paled. "Must she wear them?"

Ergon studied his master's face. "Considering their previous owner, I thought it appropriate." He raised a pale brow. "Was I wrong?"

Whispier seemed to wrestle within himself for a moment before waving a graceful hand in my direction. "We have nothing else even close to her size, I suppose."

Ergon draped a sage green silk tunic over my arm before adding a pair of tan leggings of supple moleskin. "I assume you would prefer to keep your own underthings for now."

I wordlessly nodded.

"You can change in there," Whispier ordered, waving toward what appeared to be Waldorf's office. "Give the stained garments to Ergon. He can attempt to remove the stains and repair them."

As tempted as I was to ask about the woman who had worn the clothing before me, something in Whispier's expression warned me that now was not the time. I filed the question away for later and obediently slipped into the office to change.

When I emerged from the office, marveling in the comfort of the fine materials, I found Whispier was still in the kitchen. Ergon, on the other hand, was nowhere in sight.

Whispier didn't acknowledge my reappearance. Instead, he continued his conversation with the cook. "See that you plan a diet that stimulates blood production in humans. And she must rest today."

Waldorf nodded as he chopped herbs. "She lost a great deal based on the staining." He then eyed Whispier without slowing the movement of his knife and the sharp clacking of the blade on the cutting board. "You as well."

"A minute more and she would've died." The muted horror in Whispier tone made my neck tingle.

I rubbed the spot where my skin had been warmer than usual. It spanned from my collarbone to my ear. How badly had I been injured?

"How do they fit?" His gaze flitted over my hand where it rested at the base of my throat. "Alice, my father's companion, was only slightly taller than you if I recall."

"The leggings are slightly long for me and baggy around the waist. My belt holds them up well." I frowned up at him. "What do you mean I was moments from death? How severe was my injury? Why do I have to rest today? And what gives you the right to order me around?" My anger had grown as the questions slipped from my lips.

To my great annoyance, my questions seemed to amuse the elf. His eyes lightened, and one side of his mouth quirked ever so slightly.

"I am glad to see you have lost none of your fire. All you would need to do is hurl things at my head, and I might consider beginning training you today."

"Training me?" I demanded.

Instead of answering me, his eyebrows lowered as he advanced on me. Before I could figure out what he intended, his cool fingertips brushed the underside of my jaw. Instinctively, I lifted my chin away from him, but he followed my retreat, bending closer to eye my throat.

"What are you—?"

"Hold still," he ordered, his tone turned suddenly deadly. His hand caught my chin between the length of his thumb and his splayed fingers across my cheek.

Heat flooded my face, but he ignored it.

"Does this hurt?" His fingers traced my earlobe, sending a shiver down my spine.

"No."

"Swallow."

I resisted the impulse.

"Avril, I am just checking to make sure I did an adequate job healing you. Swallow."

I complied. "I feel fine. Well, except for a slight burning sensation."

A tingle of magic caressed my skin. With it came the scents I was beginning to associate with Whispier: trees, grass, light, and warmth. They filled my nostrils with heady abandon.

"Master Whispier," I protested.

"What would Casimir say?" A new voice demanded. A woman stood just out of my field of view, hampered as I was by the hand on my jaw.

"Some comment about something that is not in his purview most likely," Whispier responded coolly to the new arrival as he released me. "Welcome back, Loriena. It is always a pleasure to see you." The ice in his tone belied the words.

Loriena stood taller than me. All elves did as far as I knew. Unlike Whispier and the men I had seen since arriving, she was dressed to perfection. Delicate silk flowed over her slender form, elegantly falling into effortless folds and drapes that emphasized the best aspects of her form. Perfectly coifed black curls cascaded over one shoulder. Where the brothers were green-eyed, her pale silver gaze held not one bit of color.

"Likewise," she murmured. Not even sparing Whispier a glance, she assessed me. "Who is the human? I heard you had obtained a new pet. I thought you had sworn off taking any more creatures into your care after what happened to the last one."

Whispier took a small step to the side, maneuvering so that I stood behind his shoulder. "Avril, this is my cousin Loriena." Every muscle in his back tensed as though he were forcing himself to do something he loathed with every molecule of his being. "Loriena, she is my companion. She is not a creature. Do not touch."

Loriena's smile was pure mischief and not of the benign variety.

My right hand, the one hidden behind Whispier's back, slid to the hilt of my knife. I had transferred it to hang openly from my belt. Thanks to the spymaster, it would probably still be a surprise when I cut her if she tried something. The cut of her gown left no room for hidden weapons, not that the elves really needed any considering I had witnessed Whispier produce and disappear things out of thin air.

"You know how I enjoy playing with your pets, Illeron," she cooed. "The last one squealed so delightfully when I scratched its face." A set of razor-tipped nails sprouted from her left hand. "And they are so vulnerable to poison."

"So, you were the one." His magic seemed to respond to his anger, seething in cloud of in sharp prickles.

"Of course." She advanced closer to me with practiced nonchalance.

Before my knife left my belt, Whispier stepped entirely in front of me, blocking all access to me as a blanket of sharply tingling magic completely enveloped the pair of us. I hastily stepped closer to Whispier's back to avoid touching the hard surface of the ward. He reached back and caught my wrist, restraining my ability to move my knife. Despite the restriction, his grip was gentle.

"My previous companion, Hiram, did nothing to hurt you." His voice had turned far too mild for comfort. The muscles in his back tensed and the ward sharpened.

"Brownies are so annoying." Loriena rolled her eyes before grinning. "I did you a favor."

Whispier muttered a word. With a series of cracks, we were surrounded by tall, dark, lethal shadow elves.

"You are no longer welcome in my home or lands. You are shunned from touching, speaking, or interacting with anything associated with me or mine. Begone."

She shrieked as one of the shadow elves grabbed her sharp-fingered hand. With a final crack, she and her guard disappeared.

"About time you did that," Casimir commented from next to me. "What did she do?"

"Confessed to killing Hiram and threatened my companion." The ward melted from around us.

I moved to step away from him, but he didn't release my hand as he continued to give out orders. Within moments the kitchen was empty again, except for the four of us. Waldorf had not paused in the preparations for the next meal the whole time. I wondered what kind of household this was where confrontations with threatening family members appeared to be a common occurrence.

"I will add her to the bans from the grounds." Casimir volunteered while observing Whispier's continued hold on my wrist.

"Please do. And see that everyone knows why."

Casimir met my gaze with a slightly raised eyebrow before silently whipping away, leaving the slightest breeze behind.

"I want my hand back," I informed Whispier.

"You can have it after you give me your weapon."

"No." I twisted my arm around so the two of us were facing each other. As difficult as it was to glare up at him and not be intimidated by his height, I was determined to try. "Since I arrived, I have been attacked by a harpy and now threatened by a woman whom you call cousin. I would prefer remaining armed for the time being."

His eyes darkened. "I only wish to examine it."

"You will give it back."

"Yes."

"Immediately."

He nodded.

"In the same condition that you received it."

He snorted. "What do you suspect I am going to do?"

"Take away my only means of defense."

"I want to make sure it is worthy." His fingers curled around mine, gently asking me to release my grip.

I doubted him, but at the same time, he hadn't lied to me yet. Besides, if he wanted to take it, he could. I held no doubts that he could have pried it from my fingers without any effort at all.

I let go.

Whispier deftly caught the weapon and stepped back to examine it.

"Plain, but solid." He ran a finger along the blade. "Cared for." He flipped it up into the air, slid it across the back of his hand, and balanced it on the end of his finger. "Well balanced." He flipped it again, catching it in his palm again before offering it back to me. "You have had this weapon for a long time."

I reclaimed my dagger swiftly so that he would not have a chance to capture my hand again. He didn't even attempt it. Instead, he moved toward our abandoned food.

"What other weapons have you trained with?"

I sheathed my dagger. "Bow, longbow, crossbow, lance, sword, knife, and spear." I listed them off for him. "Among other things."

"Who have you trained against?"

"Human, woodwose, brownie—" This earned a smile and nod from Waldorf. "—pixie, and one magus, though that wasn't a training session."

"No elves?" He glanced over his shoulder as he picked up the bread from his plate.

"I avoid elves." Realizing what I was saying, I rephrased. "I avoided elves."

Turning to rest a hip against the counter, he studied me. "Why?"

"Mainly because I didn't want to come to their attention."

His eyebrows rose, and interest glinted in his gaze. "We do tend to be an observant species, but not a malicious one." He finished off the bread and reached for an orange.

"Really?" I smirked in disbelief. "You expect me to believe that after the little demonstration a few moments ago?"

"Not all elves are like Loriena." He began peeling the orange from the rind.

I snorted.

He acted as though he didn't hear me. The pile of peelings on the counter grew. "Were you avoiding any particular elf's attention?"

"Yours."

To my surprise, this didn't faze him. "Because of your brother?"

"Yes, and…" I narrowed my gaze as I debated how much to share. "You had a hand in my parents' deaths."

His hands stilled for a moment. "The hunt in the barren lands. Your brother made the same accusation."

"You deny it?"

He lifted a remarkably calm gaze to meet my glare. "I do not deny providing the intel for that operation. However, I did not kill your parents."

"They were picked out by your intel as possibly being under the influence of the Magus Maillean. Because of this, they were dragged from our home, tortured, and then put to death." Unbidden tears blurred my eyes, but I refused to drop my fixed attention on his face. "They were innocent."

"They were." He calmly set his partially peeled orange on the countertop. "I did not mention their names in any of my reports. Neither did I mention the potential of sympathizers among the populace. That was a figment of a paranoid mind—rather Warlord Axian's mind, to be exact." He rubbed his hands on the front of his shirt. "When your brother came to me five years ago with those accusations, I investigated his claim. We hunted down Axian and confronted him with the evidence. His own people executed him."

"So, you enslaved my brother?"

He flinched. "No. Your brother needed a way to support you. He said you were old enough to be left in the care of your uncle and aunt, but they demanded that he provide for your support. I offered him a contractual exchange, service for pay."

"My uncle and aunt never received pay. They threw me out on my own when I turned eighteen, and I have been supporting myself ever since."

His head snapped up. Eyes narrowed and intensely silver, he shook his head. "No. That isn't right. The last payment was sent on time and collected as arranged. Either your uncle and aunt lied, or someone stole it along the way." He crossed to me, catching my hands in his. "I will see this righted." Then before I could respond, he strode out of the room yelling for someone.

"Elves and their contracts," Waldorf commented. "Come eat, Lady Avril. Master Whispier will see all is made right."

"I will believe it when I see it." I hoped he would, but still, it was hard to go against the distrust I had built up against his species for years.

SIX

Illeron

Despite the healer's recommendations, Avril refused to rest. I had tuned my monitoring spell so it included her. The result was that I was even more acutely aware of her whereabouts. As soon as she finished her breakfast, she climbed the stairs to my study and appeared in the doorway as I was chewing out one of the sentries, Odon, who didn't raise the alarm fast enough. As I uttered my final warning, she sagged against the door frame, far too pale for my ease.

My expression must've betrayed my concern. Odon turned to look behind himself and spotted her. I moved first, speeding around him to catch Avril before she slid farther down the door frame. Swinging her up into my arms, I glared at Odon.

"That will be all. See that the others know what is at stake."

"Understood." He eyed Avril as she struggled not to lean against my shoulder and failed. "Is she well?"

"She is still suffering the consequences of your ineptitude." I glared at him.

He knew what I meant, and my message was clear.

"He didn't do the attacking." Avril's soft protest was barely loud enough for me to hear, but Odon's sharper hearing also caught it.

"He is in the right, my lady. I am in your debt. You were injured by my incompetence." He offered her a salute before stepping into my shadow and disappearing.

She gave up on keeping her head from resting against my chest. "I am so tired."

"You are supposed to be resting," I pointed out as I carried her out through the doorway onto the landing above the entrance hall. I hesitated as I realized I only knew the general direction of her room. After I instructed Ergon to give her a place to sleep, I had left it to him to choose the location.

"But you aren't."

"Hmm?" Distracted by my thoughts, I had lost track of the conversation.

"You aren't resting." She nuzzled into my shoulder and adjusted as though seeking a more comfortable position. She must've found it. She parted her lips and let out a breathy sigh. Just like that, I was holding a sleeping human.

"For all of your professed aversion to elves, you are growing far too comfortable around me," I informed her.

She didn't respond. Her breathing settled into a rhythm that I instinctively knew was too fast. Striding back into my study, I crossed to the one upholstered piece of furniture in the room, an elegant chaise that had been my mother's. Easing Avril onto it, I arranged her so that she lay flat, and I could assess her.

Her sun-kissed skin was unnaturally pale, her lips were slightly blue-tinged, and I didn't like the limpness of her limbs. Healthy people didn't fall so deeply asleep so quickly. Claiming her wrist, I checked her pulse. The frantic flutter against my fingertips did nothing to soothe my growing worry.

Accessing my healing ability, I tapped into the spells my mother had taught me. The foremost healer among our kind, she had been the one everyone sought out when cases were complicated. I believed Avril's issue was simple blood loss, but that didn't make treating it any easier. Especially since I suspected she would fight me at every turn. The only other option was a donation of appropriate human blood, but I had no access or means to offer that to her.

I did what I could. Despite her slightly elevated pulse, it became steady. Her breathing remained regular. My healing senses couldn't find anything more to fix within her. Healing frequently took time and patience. The time I could provide. Patience would be harder to convince her to practice.

"No training for you tomorrow," I whispered to her as I smoothed stray auburn strands away from her closed eyes. "Rest and good food." Rising, I crossed to the door into my bedchamber. Fetching the thick fleece throw from the end of my bed, I returned to the study and lay it over my sleeping companion.

She didn't stir but slept on.

Retreating to the table, I plucked at my magical filing system and pulled forth my reports. Thankfully, I had a few hours of work to keep me occupied while I watched over her.

The situation at the border between the warlords Batair, Cathral, and the woodwose was far worse than I feared. The more information I gathered, the grimmer it looked. No amount of subtle manipulation would stop the inevitable war between the northern human warlords and their generally peaceful neighbors. The question was if I should try to stop it. Was it worth the risk of exposing my network? Would it destroy my connections and alliances with the other warlords? Dare I risk it?

The elves had not actively and openly acted in the affairs of the humans on a large scale for at least a century, a time of peace for my people. Initially, we feared creating more power-hungry humans desperate enough to seek unethical ways to gain magic. By withdrawing from them, we limited their access to our knowledge, skills, and us.

Humans had no natural magic. Unlike the other dominant and non-dominant species populating our world since the mass exodus from fairy an eon ago, humans depended on different skills to survive. Perceptive and instinctively interactive, humans thrived on connections, maintaining, using, and growing relationships between themselves and others. While my people were obsessive about balance, power, knowledge, and contracts, humans could be sacrificial in their decisions, even for those who were not family, even for those who did not have a hold over them. It was almost a universal species trait. The exceptions were rarer than a gargoyle who wasn't worried about the security of his eyrie or a brownie who didn't care about her home. Those types did appear among populations, but they were so rare that the general stereotype held true over ninety percent of the time.

I glanced over at the still form on my chaise lounge. Avril had curled to her side, pulled my throw up to her chin, and tucked in her feet. Only her face from the nose up and a cascade of loosely braided hair were visible. The auburn strands caught the sunlight, glowing fire and hinting at the spark in the woman they belonged to.

When Fairy became a wasteland, the humans welcomed us into their territory, at least initially. They offered land and resources and negotiated peace between the myriad species of the fae. In return, our peoples had offered healing potions, tools with magical properties, and other by-products of our natural magic. The borders between our new territories stood where they were because of those first human negotiators. It only took a few decades before we all grew greedy. Elves wanted power, the gargoyles wanted isolation, and the humans wanted more land because they multiplied thanks to their improved health. Oh, and they wanted magic.

The first magus lamia discovered that humans could gain the capability to use the magic of others. Then a century after the exodus, one learned how to drain a fae's magic and store it. They didn't care that the process tortured the victim and eventually killed them. We couldn't live without our natural magic, just like a human can't live without oxygen.

I grimaced. How I wished that hadn't been discovered.

Every human became suspected of either being a magus or allied with one. Species with natural magic held humans at a distance, suspicious of their motives and intentions. We retreated behind our borders, protecting ourselves. By doing so, we failed to help those who were attempting to stop the villains. The humans fought among themselves. A civil war split their region down the middle. The threat was isolated to the west. The remaining population struggled to survive. Meanwhile, the cancer grew.

Avril stirred on the chaise. My senses instinctively heightened. Acutely aware of her, I listened for her breathing. A strand of hair fluttered against her lips and subsided at regular intervals. I resisted the urge to rise, to physically check that she was well.

Not all humans were bad. Many of my people had forgotten that fact over the centuries. Perhaps it was our longevity and matching memories or our instinctive suspicion of everyone. Still, as a species, we tended to look down on humans. They were annoying, fragile, short-lived, and aggressive.

I watched Avril sleep for a moment. Humans, for all their flaws, possessed many virtues that Elves could benefit from learning. Loyalty, honesty, integrity, and vulnerability were the first to come to mind. Also, for all their fragility, they were surprisingly tenacious.

A gentle tap at the study door made me straighten guiltily. It wouldn't do for me to be caught watching my pet sleep. Rising, I silently crossed the room and opened the door.

Ergon stood outside. "Where do you want me to serve lunch?"

I glanced over my shoulder at the mound of fleece on my mother's chaise. "Here. I will wake her if necessary. She needs to eat."

"And drink."

I nodded, and Ergon left.

Before she woke, though, I had one task to accomplish. I checked that Avril still slept soundly before stepping out into the corridor again. Summoning Odon with a twist of magic, I waited for him to appear.

"Master," he whispered as he melted out of the shadows.

"I have a top-secret mission for you."

Odon didn't even blink. "Not a word."

"None. Not even with your fellow shadow elves. I will speak to Casimir only. He will adjust your orders accordingly."

He nodded.

"I wish you to collect intel on warlords Batair and Cathral."

"That is Lynan's assignment."

I motioned for him to keep his voice down. "It is."

"And you don't want him to know I am there."

"I want no one to know, understood?"

"If I could be so bold—"

I cut him off. "I won't disclose my reasons, but I will remind you that you are in my companion's debt. This will be a first step in repaying that debt."

Odon nodded very slowly. "Understood." He glanced into the room where Avril was stirring. Both of our ears easily picked up the sounds of her movement. "I will return within a week with all I can gather." Then he stepped into the shadows next to the door and was gone.

I stepped back into my study, leaving the door open. Ergon approached from the direction of the kitchen, and my senses told me that the shadow elves were rotating positions.

Avril pushed the fleece back from her face and blinked up at the ceiling as I approached the table again.

"Rest well?" I asked. Sorting the reports into piles, I flicked them back into storage with methodical precision.

She blinked at the sunlight outside the windows. "How long did I sleep?"

"All morning."

On cue, Ergon came through the door into the study with a waft of rich smells. Various meats, cheeses, eggs, and a bean salad, all of it was filled with the nutrients she needed to rebuild her blood supply.

"Here comes lunch," I observed as I tossed my last batch of reports into the filing system.

"On the table, Master Whispier?" Ergon inquired in his perfect house manager manner.

I resisted rolling my eyes. "Yes. Please send Casimir my way after he rises and refreshes himself."

He nodded his understanding while efficiently setting out the food and place settings.

"You worked." Avril frowned at me.

"I did."

"I thought you were supposed to rest."

"Elves heal faster than humans."

She freed her legs from the fleece. "But you healed me. Your healing took far longer than mine." Setting her feet on the floor, she began rising far too quickly.

I slipped my arm around the back of her shoulders as she wobbled. "Steady. You shouldn't be making any sudden movements for a bit."

She closed her eyes and muttered, "Elven speed."

I suspected I wasn't supposed to have heard her, so I ignored it. "Do you have a preference as to seat?"

"Facing the door." She tried to shrug off my arm. "I can walk. I am not an invalid."

"I don't want you losing more blood when you split your head open falling against the table."

If looks could inflict harm, I would have been eviscerated right there.

"Very well." I released her shoulders and retreated.

She swayed slightly after I moved away, but she didn't fall. "If I am dependent, I am dead."

"You are no longer in a warlord's service," I pointed out.

Ergon placed the last platter on the table as Avril reached her chair. He offered me and then her a shallow bow before leaving, closing the door behind him.

As she seated herself, I claimed her plate. "Any objections to any of the selections?" I asked.

She scanned the offerings and then shook her head.

"Good." I filled her plate with a portion of everything. After setting it before her, I turned my attention to my own plate. "Now eat it all, healer's orders."

"You mean your orders," she responded.

"No, I mean healer's orders. He ordered this exact menu for both of us and prescribed portions." I motioned to my very full plate. "See. I am eating the same."

She grimaced but picked up her silverware.

I bent my attention to my food. True to the healer's predictions and my own experience, I was ravenously hungry. A quick glance at my dinner companion, and I was pleased to discover she appeared to be equally eager for food.

Seven

Avril

I ate with enthusiasm. As much as I knew Whispier and the healer were correct that I needed rest and hearty food to recover from blood loss, it didn't mean his resilience was any less annoying. As I finished the last of the bean salad on my plate, I eyed the basket of rolls sitting between us.

"Don't."

I lifted my chin with a carefully formed innocent expression only to find he wasn't even bothering to look. "Don't what?" He was far too staid for his own good. Cautious, over-confident, and handsome—I never knew that it could be a romantically appealing combination.

He studiously cut his chicken. "Don't throw a roll at me."

"I was only thinking," I protested.

"And staring at the rolls."

I huffed. "Just because you know about everyone's actions and whispered secrets doesn't mean you can read my mind." I jabbed a bite of cheese with my fork and popped it into my mouth.

He set his silverware on his plate with careful precision. Wiping his mouth with his linen napkin, Whispier met my gaze across the table. "Would you care to test that theory?"

The darkening of his green eyes boded ill for me. I couldn't tell if he was angry or something else. Warm anticipation threaded through me. "No."

"If I can make you think about what I want you to, you will retire to your bed and sleep the rest of the day." One of his elegant dark eyebrows rose challengingly.

"And if I don't think of what you wish?" I frowned at him. "What will I get should I win?"

"A boon."

"Any boon?"

He nodded very slowly. "Any boon short of dissolving our binding, harming anyone, or killing anyone. And it can't go against my conscience."

"I didn't know you had one." The words flew from my lips before I considered their truth.

He flinched.

I immediately wished the words back. "No, that isn't what I meant. I am sorry. Please forget you ever heard that. I—"

He raised his hand between us, palm toward me. His head lowered and tilted to one side as though processing something, he hid his face. "Perhaps it is too soon." He picked up his fork again.

I reached across the table and claimed a roll. Whispier was so preoccupied with whatever he was thinking that he didn't comment, so I launched it at his head.

The soft roll hit him square in the forehead and landed in the center of his plate. He stilled. Then very slowly, he lifted his head. His green eyes glittered darkly so that they were almost black with the silver glinting in the depths like stars. "So, you want to make the wager?"

"Yes," I whispered before letting myself think about the repercussions. I cleared my throat before repeating it louder. "Yes."

"You are that determined not to rest?" he asked, rising from his chair. He came around the end of the table, stalking my position with a tiger-like grace. I kept forgetting he was dangerous.

I stood. Instinct told me I needed to be on my feet, but I moved too quickly. My head went light, my balance shifted, and I would have fallen if he hadn't caught me.

A strong arm encircled my waist, pulling me up against his chest. My senses settled as he leaned over me. For the first time in a very long time, I felt safe, protected. No, that wasn't true. Right before falling asleep, I had been in his arms, and I wanted that closeness again.

I reached up to touch his face, my fingertips catching on the slight scruff along his jaw. Whispier leaned into my touch. Then he kissed me. It was brief, fleeting, and equilibrium disrupting in the best way. I gripped his shoulders to anchor myself, but by then, it was over.

I buried my face against his shoulder. He continued to hold me with gentle firmness as I struggled to collect my scattered thoughts.

"I won. Now, you are going to go and rest." He picked me up, tucked my head close, and then sped through the house. Before I knew it, I was standing at the counter in the center of the kitchen, and Whispier was talking to Ergon.

"See that she stays in bed for the remainder of the day." Then he was gone.

My head swam, draining any inclination to protest as Ergon herded me off to my bedchamber. I collapsed into bed with my head whirling.

What had he meant by that? I hadn't expected him to kiss me. Not that I minded much that he had. In fact, I kind of hoped he would do it again. Still, this swirl of confusion wasn't helpful. I fell asleep while trying to make the whole situation make sense.

Illeron

As impulsive as that kiss had been, I refused to regret it.

Leaning back against the edge of the table, I signaled the first shadow elf scheduled to report to me. He appeared in the middle of my study, bowing slightly. Then he launched into a detailed summary of the activity in the northern regions where the human kingdoms mingled with the brownie and lesser fae populations.

Although the region remained reasonably stable, I suspected it wouldn't stay that way.

Once he finished, I gave him a new mission: find my companion's brother and fetch him here.

The elf bowed and left.

Casimir appeared in his place with a crack of displaced air. "What were you thinking?"

"Of what do you speak." I turned away under the guise of fiddling with the remnants of lunch. Ergon hadn't come and cleared away the leavings yet.

"You kissed your companion. You flirted with her, embraced her, and kissed her right here in your study."

"Ah, that." I picked up a roll from the basket with a slight smile.

"Don't you 'ah, that' at me! I demand to know what you have been scheming. You are playing with fire, and you better have a good reason." Casimir stalked up to glare at me, practically nose to nose.

Although we were almost the same age, I being the elder by two years, we rarely vied for dominance. More importantly, we were a team. We worked together to accomplish our goals, mainly the security and preservation of the relative peace our kingdom was enjoying. Not since childhood had we grappled. Argued? Yes. Shouted? Definitely. But we always came to an agreement.

However, as I met his angry green stare, I began to suspect we would not end this argument on the same side.

"You were the one who told me to seek out companionship," I pointed out.

"I didn't tell you to adopt the first human you came across."

"Grimore sent her to me as repayment of a blood debt." I tweaked the spell holding the toy dagger. It dropped into my hand. "What was I to do? Ignore her? Insult Grimore?"

"You don't have to flirt with her."

"I hope to do more than that."

Casimir glared at me in silence. "You would risk all we have built for a human woman, a potential weakness in our defenses."

I turned away, fingering the dagger in my hands. "I am considering it."

"Light elves don't have fated mates."

"That is true. We aren't usually ones for instant connections or quick decisions concerning our mates, but we still marry for life. Like shadow elves, we commit for the entirety of our time on earth."

"Which is all the more reason for you not to choose a human." Worry, pain, and irritation warred in my brother's usually stoic features. "I don't want you to experience what Father suffered through. He was half of himself after Mother's death. You would be half of yourself for even longer since you will be far younger than him when she dies. And she will age far faster than you. What will you do when you are still a young man in the way of our species, and she is eighty?"

"I said I was considering it." He had a good point. I would need to make the aging disparity clear to Avril should I ever decide to commit to her that way. "Some elves have married humans without bonding."

He huffed softly. "I can't see you going only halfway." Affection softened his features.

"You have a point." I crossed to the table and set down the dagger before turning back to face him. "Consider for a moment that I might want to spend the rest of her days with her or a different human woman and with all the benefits available to our species."

"Even if her death means you live a half-life for the remaining centuries of your life?"

I met his assessing gaze.

"If I ask her or another, I will do so in full knowledge of that tradeoff. We light elves love no less deeply than shadow elves."

He nodded as his gaze narrowed. “I am well aware of that. I just don’t want you to throw this connection on someone unworthy.”

I fully understood a slight against Avril and humans, in general, was not meant with malice. “And if I deem her worthy and she accepts my offer?”

He flinched. “I will accept her as your wife and my sister.”

“That is all I ask.”

“It would be asking more than you realize.” With that, he was gone.

I threw myself on the chaise lounge and buried my head in my hands.

“Are you well?” Ergon asked.

I lifted my head to find him standing over me, concern marring his features. “Avril is resting. Perhaps you should as well. It has been a trying few days.”

Rubbing my face, I realized I was tempted to take his advice. “Too much to do,” I protested. “I have to finish listening to reports and then summarize them for King Emrys. I am due in his presence at the end of the week. He requires I have a plan of action on how we can proceed with this new threat.” I closed my eyes. A war between the humans and the woodwose could devastate the north, not to mention the potential for the disconnect to spread. At best, we needed to stop the conflict before it began. In the worst-case situation, we needed to plan to contain the war's effects on the rest of the continent. I groaned.

“That bad?” Ergon asked as he began clearing away the meal.

“Worse. Unless I come up with a plan, we might end up with war waging along the border between the woodwose and the northern most warlords.” Odon would return in a few days with accurate news. Until then, I could only maintain vigilance as usual.

Pushing to my feet, I signaled the next shadow elf. She whispered through the shadows and presented herself before me. I struggled to focus on her words as she spoke about Eldarlan's eastern borders. All was well by the sound of it.

The next messenger addressed the successful tracking of one of the senior magus lamias who had just been evicted from the borders of the Magus Conglomerate. He had traveled to the north, apparently intent on establishing himself amidst the warlord-controlled regions. It made sense. Where constant conflict brewed, it would be easy for him to put down roots and gather power, especially if he could convince a warlord to support his efforts.

My stomach twisted. Warlords, in general, were willing to do anything for a price.

After five more verbal reports, I was finally able to retreat to the gymnasium for a training session. I strode into the large light-filled room to find that I wasn't the only one thinking to burn off my frustrations and clear my mind. Casimir and Maury were mid-bout with great swords, my brother's weapon of choice. The two blades repeatedly clashed as Casimir sought to find a weakness in Maury's defenses. The lack of shadows in the sundrenched room made it impossible for Casimir to use his wraithwalking abilities, but it made him no less formidable.

Unwilling to interrupt them, I set to limbering up, stretching my major muscle groups and watching my brother.

"What is bothering you?" Maury demanded after a particularly aggressive move on Casimir's part.

"A disagreement." My brother grimaced. "Again."

Just then, Maury spotted me. "No. Enough beating me up. Go expend some of your aggression on your brother." Throwing the double-handed blade to me, he began walking over to the area where the towels were stacked.

Anger flared in Casimir's eyes at the sight of me, confirming my suspicions.

"Mind abstaining from weapons?" I asked. "I have already been punctured once this week. I prefer to not experience it again for a while."

Casimir tossed his blade into the air and triggered a spell similar to my own. "What makes you think I am willing to spar with you?" His dusky, copper-toned features darkened.

"Maury is right that confronting the source of your frustration is much better than taking it out on others."

A flare of silver energy formed a fiery ball around Casimir's left fist. "You would risk it all for a woman."

I coiled my magic into a blue rope. "Risk what?"

"Our family name, our reputation, everything we have worked to build since father's death. You are risking it all." He hurled a ball of energy at me. I dashed it apart with a flick of my rope.

"You mean if I choose to bond with Avril."

"Marry, bond, align, whatever you choose to call it. She is a liability." He glared as we circled each other. "Do you really think the king is going to continue to listen to us if you bring a human into our family? She could be a magus or in league with a magus." He touched the floor with his fist, and magic fire licked across the flooring toward my feet.

Leaping the fire line, I landed closer to him. Lashing out with my rope, I coiled it around one of his ankles and pulled. He resisted.

"Since when have we made personal decisions based on what the king would think of them?" I retorted.

A blast from Casimir's energy fist hit me in the shoulder. The flash caused my skin to warm, but only slightly. We weren't fighting for real. If we had been, my clothing would've been ash, and my shoulder scorched.

"Never," my brother admitted as he attempted again to pull his foot free from my coiled rope. "But I will use any argument I can to persuade you from this path."

"Why?" I demanded. Forming a second rope, I looked for an opening, but Casimir had created a defensive ward and was attempting to work it through my first rope.

"Because it is foolish." He gritted his teeth in concentration.

I began pelting him with raisin-sized tongues of fire. They melted through his ward and landed on his skin, flaring for a moment before extinguishing.

"Nothing done in love is foolish," I protested. "You should know that. Father demonstrated that to us repeatedly as we grew up."

"Even something that will only leave you a shell?" he demanded before suddenly dropping his defenses. The pain in his eyes cut through me. We were alone in the world. For so long, it had just been the two of us fighting for our place in the world. I could completely understand his fear.

I released my hold on both ropes. The magic dissipated in a flash of sparks. "First, I never said that I was definitely doing this, only that I was considering it."

He pressed his lips tightly closed as though fighting a retort.

"Second, I have waited." At a century old, I had waited longer than most elves to select a mate. Elves were made stronger by companionship and marriage. Casimir and I were unusual in our lack of interest in bonding for so long. Truth is, neither of us had particularly wished to ally ourselves with any of the elven females we had met thus far. Thanks to our connections, we knew almost every elf in Eldarlan. We knew who was out there and available.

"We might still be the end of our line," I pointed out. "Avril could deny me if I asked. I might never make the offer." Elven courtship rituals were long and extensive. If one was committing to centuries in union with another, it made sense to be entirely sure of alignment in every way. Still, there was more to a marriage than compatibility. "It is too early to tell, but I am concerned at the strength of your objections to me even entertaining the possibility."

He looked away from me and glared at the far wall. "Just remember that you are not the only one who has to live with your decision."

"I promise I won't forget it." A slight jolt shot through me as the promise took hold.

"That is all I ask." Casimir dropped his chin to his chest. "Now, why did you send Odon to walk Lynan's region?"

EIGHT

Avril

When I woke the next morning, my stomach immediately announced it was empty. The bone-deep exhaustion had abated. Rolling to my feet, I discovered a new outfit draped across the bench at the foot of my bed. A long, delicately floaty tunic in a heather blue and another pair of soft moleskin leggings. This pair had been dyed a velvety taupe. I dressed and prepared to head to the kitchen for breakfast, but I caught a glance of myself in the mirror as I walked past.

Wait!

I backtracked a few steps. I hadn't noticed as I dressed, but this ensemble fit me perfectly. I hadn't grown in the night. I slid my hand through the slit in the softly draping layers to touch the hilt of my knife, where it hung from a belt at my waist. The colors, the cut, the secret slit, it was almost as though the clothing had been made specifically for me. I frowned at myself in the mirror. When had I been measured?

On a whim, I crossed to the wardrobe that dominated the corner of my bedchamber and opened the door. An array of options immediately presented themselves. Tunics, shirts, gowns, leggings, pants, skirts, the contents were enough to dress a royal woman for a year. I caught the sleeve of a deep green gown and confirmed my suspicion. The fabric quality alone made each of these worth a fortune.

I frowned. When did Whispier think I would ever be wearing a ball gown? I never wore dresses or skirts because they tended to hamper my motions and create excessive noise. They created two potentially deadly flaws when one was trying to go unnoticed. Still, my fingers lingered. I couldn't help appreciating the softness and the beauty. I dropped the skirt and closed the door. No matter how pretty it was, I couldn't accept it. Spymaster or not, Whispier would not be spoiling me.

I stalked off toward the kitchen.

The corridors were unusually still, even for the typical quiet. No shadow elves stepped from shade to shadow, inclining their heads in my direction as they passed. No whispers or shuffling of servants, which I had come to expect on my walk from my bedchamber to fetch my breakfast every morning.

I glanced at the nearest window. Perhaps it was late in the morning, and I had overslept.

When I reached the kitchen, I found Waldorf perched on a stool and reading a recipe book. "Ah, you are awake." He flashed me a grin before hopping off the seat and pulling out a cutting board and knife. "Do you prefer a sandwich or some hearty stew? I served Master Whispier his lunch an hour ago."

"Whichever is less preparation." I glanced at the window again. Afternoon? I had slept a very long time. My stomach growled.

"Hmm…" Waldorf waved a hand toward my stomach. "I suspect you will need both, considering the volume of your stomach and the fact that you slept through three meals."

"My apologies for not waking for dinner."

He shook his head as he dug out a bowl. "Nonsense! You needed your sleep. Besides, Whispier left orders for you to rest undisturbed for as long as you needed." The brownie flashed me another smile. "The house has been abuzz."

"Why?" I rested my elbows on the counter to watch him work.

"Maintenance of the wards was moved forward after the incidence with the harpies. Also, Whispier called for a debriefing of the staff in anticipation of an increase of security."

"Is that why the corridors are strangely quiet this afternoon?"

Waldorf nodded. "He has all the shadow elves strengthening the wards, and the staff should be finishing up their meeting with him any minute."

It was a great deal of fuss for a single attack. Grimore's stronghold was regularly attacked by other warlords and herds of unicorns, harpies, goblins, and occasionally lone chimeras. The attacks were inevitable and rarely required such a massive effort to increase security.

I stole a piece of cheese. "Why all the effort?"

Waldorf paused in cutting the bread for my sandwich to frown at me in concern. "We have never had an attack of this nature make it past the perimeter of the grounds, let alone reach the palace." The brownie shivered. "Whispier is determined it won't happen again."

"The benefits of magic, I suppose."

Waldorf considered me gravely. "What do you mean?"

I shrugged. "The warlords have to rely on physical means to hold off attacks. Obstacles like thick stone walls, thick beam lattices, constant vigilance, and ready warriors were our only defenses. Most attacks reached our walls, and only occasionally they were breached." I gestured in the direction of the window behind me. "Windows are a dangerous luxury, and foregoing heavy fortifications outside the walls would be an invitation to death."

Waldorf gravely nodded. "I have never been more thankful for Master Whispier's and the elves' efforts. I have never lived outside this residence. After hearing that, I have no wish to stray." He shivered slightly. "The warlord's region sounds barbaric."

"It is." There was no shame in admitting the truth. As he prepared my meal, I gave him an extended summary of my observations of the world beyond the elven borders.

He listened with rapt attention, asking insightful questions. How did we grow food? Where did we get our weapons? How had I trained to be a thief?

I explained the drilling and practice I had been taught to keep my steps light, movements fluid, and fingers nimble. He was fascinated.

When I finished eating, he sent me off in the direction of the library. Apparently, the significant repairs had already been completed. Whispier had moved his work area back in there.

However, as I approached the library, a commotion broke out in the entrance hall. Raised voices and a thump that could only be someone hitting a wall demanded I investigate. I hurried past the library door and ran for the foyer. Skidding to a halt just inside the doorway, I was stunned to see my brother wrestling with a shadow elf.

"I demand to see Whispier!" He growled as he gripped the elf's wrist, which was how the elf was pinning him to the wall. His feet dangled a solid foot above the floor, feet flailing in his effort to escape the elf's hand splayed across his chest.

"Solon?" I asked.

My brother's fiery red head swiveled. His brown eyes widened. "Avril! A little help here?"

I eyed the shadow elf. "Dargan?"

He surveyed me with a glint of amusement in his light-colored eyes. "Do you have a request, my lady?"

"Don't kill him."

Dargan's eyes lightened in what I had begun to understand was a sign of amusement in an elf. "I mean him no harm. I am merely defending myself."

"Really." Solon sputtered. "You started it with abducting me."

Dargan regarded Solon coolly. "You requested that I bring you to Master Whispier when I informed you that he had contracted your sister as a companion."

"I never gave you permission to take me with you through shadows like a wraith. Neither did I agree to manhandling."

"You pulled a knife on me."

I scanned the floor, spotting my brother's favorite blade glinting on the rug in the center of the room. "Do you have any more weapons?" I asked Solon.

My brother snorted. "Like I would say in front of this thug."

"My lady, if you would?"

I crossed to the knife, picking it up. "Confiscated," I informed Dargan.

"Throw it here," Solon demanded, extending a hand in my direction.

"What do you mean to do with it?" I asked.

"Carve that meddling, backstabbing spymaster a reminder of his betrayal, preferably in the middle of his chest." His eyes narrowed in on Dargan. "But first, I intend on teaching this bully a lesson."

"In that case, I am going to have to hold onto it."

That caught Solon's attention. "Say what?"

"You see, I made a vow."

Solon cursed. "He made you trade places." He cursed again before arching his back and bellowing as best he could, considering he was pinned to the wall by a very patient shadow elf. "Whispier!"

"No need to yell." The calm voice came from directly behind me. I had not heard his approach, but I strangely wasn't surprised when he ran his fingers along my arm, caressing the inside of my wrist as I released the knife into his hold. "Thank you," he whispered in my ear before stepping around me to face Solon. "Release him, Dargan."

Dargan slid Solon down the wall until his feet touched the floor and then released him.

Solon rubbed his chest as he straightened to his feet. "I have a complaint to register with you, spymaster."

"So, I have heard. In fact, I suspect my whole household heard. We elves have sensitive hearing if you recall."

"I do." Solon took a deep breath and then groaned. "Did you really have to punch me in the ribs?" he complained at Dargan.

"You cut me." The shadow elf made the statement without emotion.

"Sounds like a reasonable response to me," Whispier commented. "This your blade?" He held up the knife.

"It is."

"I will return it to you later. What is the matter you wish to discuss with me?"

Solon glared. "You tricked my sister into a bait and switch."

"I offered her a place as my companion, and she accepted."

"Why would she?" My brother waved toward me. "I was providing for her. When we made our agreement, you promised to send money."

"There was no money," I commented.

"What!" Solon adjusted his stance as though readying for a fight. "So, you are a cheat as well as a backstabber."

"She was sent to steal from me by Grimore, her current employer. Once I realized who she was and what she wanted, I offered her a solution." Whispier calmly turned to me. "We negotiated terms. She accepted. Have I upheld my end of our agreement?" he asked.

"You have." Carefully keeping my expression neutral despite the sudden memory of his kiss the night before, I glanced at Solon's flushed features. The anger in his eyes hadn't dimmed in the least. "I bargained for your freedom in exchange for companionship. So far, I have been very well cared for and protected. He even tolerates my teasing."

Whispier's green gaze warmed as he studied my face and the corner of his mouth lifted ever so slightly. "I did tell you that you were welcome to annoy me. You are only fulfilling the contract."

"By launching rolls at your head?"

A soft smile spread across his face. After the impassive mask I had grown accustomed to, the smile was blinding. "Among other things."

"Wait!" Solon took a step toward Whispier, but Dargan moved to intervene with a raised hand. Solon immediately stepped back again, rubbing his chest. "Let me get this right. You sent money to my sister, and she never received it?"

Whispier's amusement disappeared instantly. "Exactly."

Solon stared at me in blank horror. "So, you have been…."

"Well," I insisted. "Once our Aunt threw me out of the house, I sought out work. Grimore was hiring thieves. All I had to do was pass a test, and I was hired."

"What test? You aren't a thief."

"They trained me." I met Solon's worry with a smile. "I am the best of Grimore's resources when he needs something acquired."

"Were," Whispier clarified. "You are no longer working for Grimore."

I rolled my eyes at him. "Fine. I was. Happy?"

"Satisfied," he responded.

Solon's gaze flicked from Whispier to me and back as though he had just realized something. "And the money?"

Whispier tensed. "The situation will be rectified in time."

Solon narrowed his glare. "When?"

"I am investigating. Have you ever known me to leave things undone?"

To my surprise, Solon accepted this with a brief nod.

Whispier met Dargan's frown with a grimace of his own. "Of more immediate concern is the fact she is being targeted."

"By whom?" Solon demanded.

"Why?" I asked. "Why would anyone want me dead?"

The spymaster studied my brother's blade. "I intend to find out."

NINE

Avril

Solon stayed in the palace. After instructing Ergon to assign my brother the room next to mine, Whispier disappeared into his study without further comment.

"What possessed you to try and steal from an elf?" Solon demanded the moment we were alone in his bedchamber.

"It wasn't as though I did it willingly," I protested. "I returned from the raid on Ohata's fortress with the team, and Grimore pulled me aside. He said it was a personal mission. Apparently, he thought I was the only one suitable for it."

Recalling the warlord's phrasing and expression in hindsight, I began to suspect Grimore had known that Whispier would catch me, and I wouldn't be returning. Strange to think I might have been a final piece in some strange blood oath agreement between the warlord and the elf. I would have to pin Whispier down and have him explain at some point.

"Sneaky geezer," Solon muttered. "First, Grimore drives me out, and then he exploits you."

"He didn't." I glared at my brother before crossing to the window.

"Drive me out or exploit you?" Solon tossed his cloak over the nearest chair.

I made a face at him. "Both. Either. You decided to run off on your own, remember. He had nothing to do with it."

"Not true." Solon began removing his extra weapons from their various places on his person. "I petitioned him for help first. The miser refused me a decent wage in exchange for my service."

I rolled my eyes. "Really, Solon. You were fifteen. How many boys that young are skilled enough to demand a wage, any wage?"

"I had been training," he protested. "Besides, he had a duty to us after our parents' faithful service. Not to mention how they died." He swung around with a glare. "Do you know what he told me? He said he had already paid our parents risk compensation, and he couldn't help it if we had already spent it. Arrogant miser!"

A niggling suspicion had been bothering me for months now. It had taken more clarity the longer I spent with Whispier. I suspected our aunt and uncle were responsible for the missing funds. "The spymaster is an honorable elf."

Solon paused in arranging his weapons. "Yeah, so?"

"He wouldn't lie."

Solon shrugged. "He is incapable of it. Light elves can't lie, and even the shadow ones are physically disturbed if they do. Something about their brain chemistry. Malida tried to explain it to me once."

"Malida?" I asked.

"A shadow elf in our squad, she did the scouting and such ahead of our infiltrations. She was annoyed by my ignorance and tried to explain things to me." His demeanor had shifted toward the dismissive, but I wasn't fooled.

Amusement made me smile.

"What?" Solon demanded. "What is with the smile?"

I shook my head and stored the possibility of him having an elf girlfriend away for later. I would tease him about it when he least expected it. "My point is that Whispier wouldn't cheat us, either of us, right?"

Solon nodded.

"Then he most likely sent the money. I suspect both Grimore and Whispier sent the money they said they did."

"So, you are saying our aunt and uncle lied?"

"I suspect they collected it all and decided not to mention it to us."

Anger flared in Solon's eyes. "How soon after I left did they toss you out the door?"

"A week at most." That time had been a blur of pain, grief, and then panic when suddenly I was without a home, family, or a means of support.

I grimaced. "I suspect Grimore also sent the support to them, and they never mentioned it. He is an honorable man for a warlord. He didn't have to offer me a chance, a way to survive with honor."

"He exploited an opportunity." Hefting his gear onto the bed, Solon surveyed the room. "I keep forgetting how rich Whispier is." He pulled his satchel closer and began unpacking his weapons. "Is the gymnasium still available to anyone?"

"As far as I know." I hadn't had an opportunity to utilize the space yet. "I have only visited it in Whispier's company."

"I am going to go train." He reached for his gear bag again.

"I should probably go find Whispier."

Solon snorted. "Right, you have a position now and a duty to keep him company."

"I am his companion."

Solon waved me off with a grimace. He clearly wasn't happy about the arrangement, but there was nothing he could do about it. I had committed myself, and I was determined to see it through. Besides, the spell agreement bound me.

Slipping out into the corridor, I headed toward the library only to be waylaid by a shadow elf. He materialized in the shade of a giant fern against the wall farther down the hallway. His coppery skin was marked by scars, and the dark hair falling about his ears was highlighted with silver strands. He turned to regard me with golden-toned eyes that glowed slightly.

"Mistress Avril." He greeted me with a gravelly tone.

"Master elf," I replied as I had done to every elf I could not name when they greeted me. I continued to walk past him.

"If I could speak with you?"

"Of course." I motioned for him to come closer, but he didn't immediately join me. Turning to look over my shoulder, I glimpsed an expression I had never seen on an elven face. He was nervous. I stopped and turned to face him. "I am listening."

His eyes lightened as a slight lifting of the corners of his mouth hinted at a smile. "As you may know, shadow elves are different than light elves."

A small laugh escaped me. "I know very little of your kind. Aside from the obvious differences, I am in the dark on many aspects of your species." I met his serious regard with a warm smile. "However, I am eager to learn."

The skin of his cheeks flushed a slightly deeper tone. "Unlike light elves, shadow elves have an instinctive reaction to females, one particular female. It only happens once in our lifetime, as far as we know. For lack of a better way of describing it, we know within moments of meeting someone that they are our match."

"Sounds life-changing," I studied the large male in front of me.

He nodded gravely. "As far back as our recorded history, this has only happened between an elven male and female." He paused.

"But?" I prompted, already fearing his next words.

"If it should happen between an elf and a human, how would a human female respond to—" He swallowed. "Should an elf declare himself to a human, would she be open to the possibility of such a commitment?" He searched my features. The vulnerability in his eyes contrasted sharply with his stoic expression.

"It depends on the woman. Should that happen, I would recommend the elf go slowly. Humans who believe in instantaneous attachment are few and far between. Should the woman not be one of those, she will require very gentle convincing."

He nodded slowly. "But there would still be hope?"

"Yes, I would guess so." As I studied the fearsome and hardened warrior before me, I couldn't help wishing to meet the woman who had captured his heart. "Do light elves have quirks of their own that they don't share with shadow elves?"

"They are obsessed with truth and knowledge." He quirked an eyebrow. "We are a race of strong emotions, but our lighter brothers tend to be more open in their expression of them. We both prefer forthright dealings when it comes to our familial relationships. They place more emphasis on balance and give and take than we do. Oh, and they are far superior healers than most of us."

Good to know. I tucked that away for later. "Was there anything else you would like to ask?"

"No, thank you, Lady Avril." He bowed slightly. "Should you need anything, call on me. I am in your debt." He stepped into a shadow and was gone before I could point out that he never gave me his name.

Reaching the library doorway without further interruption, I found the door open. Whispier sat at the table in the center of the room, his back to the door. My usual place in what I had come to realize was his favorite chair stood empty. One of the servants had mentioned it in passing while he was cleaning the room when I lingered in there alone.

Whispier's curly dark head bent over the pages of notes. His broad, solid shoulders filled out the fine blue cotton of his shirt. I admired the line of them as he scribbled something down. How had I ended up here? Solon's questions had brought up all the complex feelings of the past. My fear of starvation, the grueling fight for respect and courtesy, and Grimore's distant and almost fatherly affection all crowded for my attention. The sinking feeling over never being good enough followed close behind. My aunt had said I was too loud. My uncle complained that I cost too much. While Solon had been home, his fierce brotherly love had been enough to keep me anchored. But once he left, I had struggled with feeling adrift.

"Have you come to hurl things at my head again?" Whispier asked in a tone that made me smile, despite the melancholy squeezing of my heart. "Do I need to defend myself?" He rose, shuffling through the pages as he did so. Pulling out one from the mess, he flicked it into his magical filing system.

I loved his quiet and expert efficiency. If only the whole world could be so perfectly organized.

"Why do you tolerate me?"

He turned to face me in a slow, liquid movement, almost as though he feared I would spook like a horse. "Why wouldn't I? You are a delight." His perceptive green gaze studied my features with concern.

Moisture flooded my eyes. I blinked back the threatening tears. How could one person be so consistently kind? Within moments, he was standing over me. Cradling my face in his hands, Whispier wiped away the few tears that escaped.

"What is wrong? Did your brother hurt you? Did he say something?"

I shook my head within the cradle of his palms. "Solon didn't do anything wrong."

His brows lowered, and his mouth tightened. "Are you certain? Your brother can be harsh at times."

I closed my eyes with a small laugh. That was an understatement. Solon had the tact of a raging minotaur. "Our conversation brought up some painful memories, that is all." I lifted my gaze to him again. Awareness tickled my senses as I realized how close he was standing. His breath caressed my forehead as he pulled me into a gentle embrace.

Surrounded by warmth and the firm pressure of his arms around my shoulders and back, my tension eased. My arms came around him as I pressed my palms against his back, keeping him there. I buried my face against his chest and breathed deeply of the scents of contentment, of him. Instead of putting distance between us, he tightened his embrace with a soft murmur. His lips brushed my forehead.

"All will be well," he whispered against my ear. "You are safe."

Part of me wished I could believe him. For the moment, I let myself dream that he spoke the truth. For a precious moment, I leaned into that thought and relaxed.

Then he stiffened. Muttering something in elvish, he kissed my forehead again. "Sorry, love." He strode across the room toward the open door as the sound of voices and approaching footsteps reached my ears. In a smooth motion, he closed the door before turning back to assess me with an intense mossy stare.

The voices passed the door.

"I think it is time you call me Illeron." His voice was low and slightly husky.

"Why?" I asked.

"Because I wish to kiss you again, and I want to make sure it is done on equal terms."

"Illeron." I tested the sound of it.

He smiled. It began as a quirk of his mouth, but then it widened. "What do you think?"

I tilted my head to the side. "What does it mean?"

"Secret keeper." He pushed off from the door and approached.

"It sounds strangely appropriate."

He shrugged. "My father was a spymaster before me. He hoped I would take his place." He reached out and stroked my chin. "May I?"

"Will it unbalance our agreement?"

"Only if you object."

My attention focused on his mouth for a moment, remembering the previous kiss and his wager.

"No objection."

He spanned the distance between us in a single step, pulled me into his arms, and kissed me.

Ten

Illeron

To my surprise, Casimir didn't immediately confront me about Avril the next morning during his debrief of the events of the previous night's activities. We stood in my study.

"Blagden brought news from Goring. The southern warlords are making noises about elven infringement on their lands. I sent him to speak with the king of the eastern elder lands and inquire about the enforcing of the treaties." Casimir rotated his head cautiously as though his neck muscles ached. "Of more concern is the news from the far north beyond the mountains. The Unseelie have begun their wild hunts again. By all accounts, they have trampled multiple fields along the borders of their forest since spring. Of even more concern is the fact young women have been disappearing during each hunt. You might want to speak with the Seelie King and soon."

Studying my brother, I asked, "When was the last time you slept adequately?"

He shrugged. "I get enough sleep. It is all of this running about that you require of me these days. It is sapping my strength. I won't object to being asked to sit."

I motioned to Avril's usual chair. "Has there been a disruption in the ranks?"

"Regarding the increased workload? No." Dropping into the chair next to the one I had indicated, he jutted his chin toward her chair. "Where is your companion this morning?"

"In the gardens. Avril said goodbye to her brother when he left this morning and then needed some time and space." I walked to the window and scanned the ordered paths. "I sent her out to walk. It will help strengthen her." Her auburn hair was easy to spot among the hedges. The sunlight caught the highlights, burnishing it with a fiery glow.

"How is her recovery coming?"

"Not as swift as I would like."

"Wishing you could manufacture blood for her?" Casimir's tone held no malice, but I glanced over my shoulder at him to check his features.

Finding only genuine concern in his stoic features, I nodded. "She is stronger than she looks, but humans are so —"

"Fragile. You have mentioned that before." His gaze narrowed. "I take it by your activities yesterday that you are set on your course."

I turned back to gaze out on the sun-dazzled garden. "How do you know when you find your other half?"

The chair creaked as he shifted. "You mean your heartmate? I wouldn't know since I haven't experienced it yet." He rose and came to stand behind my shoulder. "Are you sure?"

Avril had paused to speak with one of the gardeners. The gnome stared up at her in rapt attention as she asked her question. Then when he answered her, she laughed. Jealousy flared. I had yet to hear her genuinely laugh. Intense longing for that sound caught me by surprise.

"An insatiable hunger to be near her, know her, and see she is safe, well, and happy," Casimir said from beside me. "One described it that way. Another said it was that she was his home and brought him peace. Seems a bit overblown if you ask me."

I wasn't as confident. Light elves weren't supposed to recognize their future mates on sight, but I had felt a connection with Avril from the beginning.

"Especially for a connection with such a fragile being," Casimir muttered.

"You aren't going to start that again, are you?" I asked ominously as I strode away from the window. "It is my decision."

"Ah, but it is her decision as well."

I smirked at the idea of Casimir trying to change Avril's mind on anything. "Any other reports for me?"

"Only the written ones." He turned to motion at the table where he had stacked the papers.

"I will see to them." I glanced at him. "Go get some sleep before you fall over."

Casimir nodded and yawned. "Behave."

I snorted. "Unlikely."

He departed quietly, leaving me to silence and work.

Avril found me there when she bounded in from the gardens. Her step light, I could hear her as she practically danced up the stairs from the conservatory. She burst into my study like a ray of sunlight, bringing warmth and the earthy smells of life. The air behind me stirred with her passing. She walked around me on the way to her usual perch on the upholstered chair facing the door.

"Did you know your gardener is witty?" She sat down as I looked up. After settling herself, she lifted an expectant expression to meet my observation. "Did you?"

"I didn't," I admitted, drinking in her smile. "I haven't had the opportunity to discuss much with him beyond the plantings and how they interfered or assisted in security."

A puzzled frown pulled at her mouth as she studied my features. "Have you ever walked the gardens?"

"I am generally too busy." I dropped my attention to the list of actions I was compiling for Casimir to review so we could discuss them. "Too much to do in too little time."

She appeared to accept this, until suddenly she was at my side, looking over my shoulder. "What is so pressing?"

I lifted my head, nearly bumping my forehead against her chin before I met her gaze. "What do you mean?"

"I wish to understand exactly what you are doing."

"I am safeguarding the security of our world."

"Sounds a bit lofty to me." She studied my list. Her hand rested on my shoulder. As she leaned forward, her thick braid of orange-scented hair slid over her arm and brushed my sleeve, the end coming to rest on the back of my hand.

"I only speak the truth." I caught the end of her braid, stopping it from tickling me. The curls slipped between my fingers, the hair so soft and silky. "The information we collect is shared with our allies and used against those who seek to harm them and any innocent."

"Are there always so many reports?" She withdrew and picked up the list I had been preparing.

"Not always. Nefarious activity has increased. Discontent among the warlords in the north, the resuming of the Wild Hunt outside Unseelie lands, and now there are rumors of unrest in the south as well." I rubbed my right eyebrow. "I have been summoned by the king of Eldarlan. I am to appear before him tonight, and I have to have a plan before then."

Avril lowered the list and regarded me solemnly over the top of it. "You can't do it all."

I laughed wryly. "I will do my best."

"No, I mean it." She set the list on the top of my stacks and turned to face me. With her standing and me sitting, her chin could've rested on my forehead. I had to look up slightly to meet her gaze. "One man…elf cannot do this alone. Surely there must be someone who can assist you."

"Many do. Hundreds of elves, allies, and spies help. How do you think I get all of this?" I waved to the reports.

"No, I mean assist with the filtering and organizing of the information. Trying to ascertain what is vital from the dross of 'this king decided to eat this for breakfast' is something that a well-trained assistant could do."

"But sometimes those details are important," I protested. "Changes in habits can hint at deeper issues."

"And who knows these details beside you?"

"Casimir consolidates the reports."

"What about the verbal ones?"

"He doesn't listen to those."

"And if something happens to you?" she asked.

"Are you threatening me again?" I responded in an effort to ease the growing tension in my gut.

She sighed heavily. "No." A flash of grief flickered in her expression before she turned away to survey my mess. "I just want to help. You should be free to walk your own garden paths occasionally." She evaded my questing hand and walked back to her place.

I picked up my list again and tried to think of additional possibilities. My mind wouldn't focus. It fixated on Avril's last point. She was correct. All it would take was for me to die or be severely injured, and our whole nation's safety would be hampered. Not paralyzed—I wasn't that vital—but it would definitely be difficult for the king and others to make critical decisions without the information I processed and passed on daily. The analyst in me couldn't ignore the risk our current setup exposed us to.

Dropping the page to the table, I leaned back in my chair. How could I fix it? Who could I trust with so much power and responsibility? I would have to find someone quick, efficient, and reliable. Trustworthiness was a must. Not just someone I was comfortable with, but also someone the king approved of. I needed to discuss it with him at our meeting.

My attention strayed to my companion. She sat cross-legged in the upholstered chair with her head bent over another historical tome. This one focused on the gargoyles and their culture. It was strange that the very companion I had acquired in response to his complaint only further emphasized Casimir's point. I was lonely and a workaholic.

"You are right," I muttered.

Avril's head rose. She regarded me with slightly unfocused eyes, still clearly thinking of the book in her lap. "Pardon?"

"I do need help. The fact I haven't provided a backup for myself is a flaw in the system. It exposes us to unnecessary risk. I shall start rectifying that tonight."

"Good." She smiled, brightening the room and easing the tension in my chest.

Fighting the impulse to abandon my work and kiss her again, I nodded perfunctorily instead. She returned to reading, and I to my work.

Avril

The tension in Illeron's shoulders made my own ache in sympathy. His chocolate curls were tussled from the many times he ran his hands through them as he thought. If he rubbed his eyebrows one more time, they might disappear.

I suppressed a worried sigh. He worked too hard. Despite his protests and grumblings whenever anyone pointed it out, it was the truth. Over the weeks I had observed him and learned his habits, I had grown into agreement with his brother.

Casimir picked an argument with Illeron at least once a day about his workaholic tendencies. Considering the efficiency with which Illeron blew off his brother's concerns, I suspected this daily pestering had been going on for years. And it wasn't Casimir's only repeated topic. Apparently, Illeron's loneliness had been a perpetual sore spot between the brothers until I had shown up to steal the useless dagger. The spymaster had seen the opportunity to annoy his brother by making me his companion.

I shifted the book in my lap.

Illeron glanced my way, but I pretended to read. In truth, I was mulling over things.

I waited until he shifted his attention back to his work before daring to glance at him again.

Illeron was handsome. True, most elves were. It was something about their genetics, their magic, or something like that. I had seen many impossibly attractive male elves since taking up my role. But, Illeron triggered more of a response, an awareness, than any of the others. Perhaps it was because I was partial to the short brown hair that barely hid the pointed tips of his ears. Or, I had a soft spot for workaholics.

I laughed softly to myself.

The spymaster glanced my way and then quickly returned to his scribbling.

I had never thought of myself as a romantic. Growing up in rough circumstances, losing my parents so young, Solon leaving, and then fending for myself all drove sentimentality out of me. But deep inside, I still remember believing in the stories of true love my mother told me when I was small. Part of me had always longed for someone to love me enough to stay.

I eyed the elf farther down the table. Well, that was quickly turning into a longing for one particular elf to love me.

"Is there something on my face?" Illeron didn't look up when he spoke.

"Your hair is standing up."

He lifted his head at that.

I grinned cheekily at him.

He huffed slightly. His green eyes flared silver fire before he turned away.

I was reasonably sure I knew what that expression meant. He wanted to kiss me again. The temptation to inform him point blank that I would welcome it was intense. However, I knew that would end in his denying it. That strong thread of duty and self-restraint that made him perfect for his position would hold him back.

But he needed a break. It was evident in every line of his body. The tension hampered his productivity.

Wasn't it my purpose as his companion to help?

My gaze fell on the small bouquet that the gardener had given me and the collection of pebbles from one of the fountains. I had discarded them on the table before me.

Before I could think better of it, I reached out, picked up the smallest pebble and slid it across the tabletop until it encountered the first pile of pages. It came to an abrupt stop.

Illeron didn't look up, but his pen paused. Then it resumed scratching across the paper.

I slid the second pebble harder. It skidded under a stack of pages.

With the third one, I attempted a bouncing approach. I landed against Illeron's left sleeve.

He ignored it.

Now wholly committed to getting a rise out of him, I tossed the next one. My aim veered off. I winced.

The small pebble beaned him on the head and then fell onto the page directly in front of him. It came to rest inches from where his long fingers splayed across the paper, holding it steady.

Suddenly, it felt like the air had disappeared from the room.

He stared at the pebble for barely a second before closing his fingers around it. "Are you trying to kill me?"

"Of course not." I offered a snarky grin, but he wasn't looking. Instead, he studied the stone.

"Then why the missiles?"

"I am bored."

He straightened in his chair and turned to eye me. "You seem to have a misunderstanding about our arrangement. You are here to keep me company, not for me to entertain you."

"Ah, but you said I could annoy you."

He sighed without conviction. "And you have been exercising that right with concerning frequency."

I smirked at him. "It entertains me."

His eyes darkened to the mossy green that promised what I sought, but without the flare of silver that almost guaranteed that I would get it.

"Take a break. Only a few minutes won't hurt." I prompted because that was more important than kisses.

"Fine." He stood. "But only a few moments."

"Good!" I set aside the book and leaped to my feet. "What shall we do?"

"Someone was suggesting I take a walk in my gardens."

"Definitely good advice." I shelved the book, and he cleared the table. When I returned, I caught him pocketing the pebbles.

"Ready?" he asked.

"Yes. You won't regret this," I assured him as I led the way.

He muttered something I didn't catch, but when I turned to ask him, he motioned for me to precede him.

Heart light at the prospect of his undivided attention, I had to slow my steps to a more sedate pace as I approached the stairs. But before I could descend, he caught my hand. Lacing his fingers through mine, he brought it up so he could kiss the back of my hand. "Now, which door should we take?"

Ignoring the sharp twist of eager delight, I smiled up at him and tugged him toward the conservatory. "Come. I want to show you the frog pond. Gnoble, his name has a silent G, you know, says he counted twenty frogs there this morning. I told him I was certain I had seen more than that." I pulled Illeron out into the sunlight. "Will you help me count them?"

He did. I kept him out in the gardens for two hours before the arrival of a shadow elf called him back to work.

Eleven

Avril

Three weeks passed. I managed to cajole Illeron into the gardens at least every other day.

Casimir seemed to approve of the change. He actually smiled at me one day when I was pestering Illeron about how under-exercised I was. As his pet, I needed regular walks in the garden, or I was liable to cause trouble and destroy things.

Although the news pouring in through his various spies did not improve, Illeron appeared less stressed than before my campaign. The elf king had approved Illeron's plans for hiring an assistant. In fact, he demanded Illeron hire two because it would ease the flow of communication and offer even greater security. Hiring the assistants was taking far longer. The candidates had to be reliable, honest, organized, above reproach, and meet a whole host of additional requirements set forth by Illeron, Casimir, and the elven king.

The arranging of the meeting with the Seelie king had also run into difficulties. The Seelie king had apparently been cursed by the king of the Unseelie court. The restrictions of the curse put limits on when he could leave his realm and by whom he could be seen.

So, a meeting in the cool of the evening on the last night before a full moon was arranged. Illeron banished me from his study as the sun began to set. I didn't catch all the details, but those I did included something about a human woman being the means of breaking the curse. Illeron decided this meant I needed to be out of sight.

So, I enjoyed a delightful dinner in the kitchen, during which Waldorf chattered about his latest recipe book and all the concoctions he wished to try. After this, I slipped into the gardens as the sun released its last grip on the sky and night settled in earnest around the estate.

The gardens were almost as beautiful at night as they were during the day. Tiny lights powered by magic lined the hedges. Strategically placed glowing plants offered further light so the paths were clearly lit.

Wandering toward the frog pond, I drew my shawl tightly around my shoulders against the subtly cooling breeze. The midnight blue fleece trimmed in silver-gray had been a gift from Illeron, along with the rest of my wardrobe. Unlike the rest of my new clothing, the shawl had clearly been made for someone taller than me. The ends fell past my knees, and the middle effortlessly draped my back from shoulders to hip.

Blagden appeared in one of the shadows. "Greetings, Lady Avril." He inclined his head to me. "Pleasant evening for a walk." He glanced about. "No, Master Whispier?"

Despite our rough beginning, he had warmed to me over the past few weeks. I glanced up at him. "Illeron had something of importance to attend to this evening. I decided a walk would be the perfect end to the evening. The gardens are so lovely."

The elf scanned the landscape once again with a more considering gaze. "They are." He offered me a weak smile. "I suppose I have always passed through them with far too much haste to appreciate it."

We stood in companionable silence for a few moments before he bowed to me. "I must depart. I wish you a good evening, Lady Avril. May you have a pleasant walk."

"Thank you."

Then he was gone.

The moon rose over the palace. Its glow waxed and waned as the clouds blew across the sky. I reached the pond and perched on the bench in the shadow of a towering pine. Floating globes of light hovered above the water, casting a silvery glow to the ripples caused by the breeze. It created an intricate play of shadow and light.

How quickly all this beauty had become comfortable. Only a matter of weeks in the past, I had been creeping through this exact garden with the intent to steal. Like Blagden, I hadn't taken the time to appreciate the landscaping, the quiet, the tranquility. I drew in a deep breath. So much had changed since then.

A soft gust of air signaled the arrival of a shadow elf behind me.

"Convenient," he muttered. Grabbing my shawl, he dragged it down, baring the back of my left shoulder to the cool air. Then with a vicious slash, he ripped a blade through the cloth and deep into my shoulder. I gasped in pain and surprise.

Instinct finally kicked in as I scrambled to pull the blade I still carried, but I was too slow. He was gone. I hadn't even been able to identify him.

A violent crack of rushed air whipped my hair into my face. I raised my good arm and fisted dagger, ready to defend myself, but the new arrival caught my wrist in his dark hand. "Lady Avril?"

Relief flooded through me. I knew him. It was the scarred shadow elf with the silver-streaked hair. I didn't know his name, but I instinctively trusted him. I dropped my knife and sagged to my knees as I struggled with a sudden wave of pain. A warm rush of blood coursed from my wound as tears threatened.

"I was attacked," I managed. "It was a shadow elf."

The elf standing over me tensed.

Suddenly, the crack of an angrily arriving shadow elf interrupted me. Followed by Illeron's voice. "If you weren't my brother—"

I didn't need to lift my head to know who had transported Illeron—Casimir.

"Avril." Illeron knelt so closely that I could feel the heat of him. A shiver jolted through me, bringing with it a fresh flare of pain. His warmth surrounded me as he pulled me close. It more than made up for the pain. I willingly leaned into his solid reassurance, breathing deeply of his familiar scent.

"It is deep," Casimir observed with a foreign note of concern in his voice.

Illeron's warm hand settled over my wound, and the tingle of healing magic permeated my shoulder.

I lifted my head to meet his gaze at just the right moment to see the air behind him begin to glow and waver. Then, the very fabric of the world seemed to rip in two. Through the tear, I glimpsed part of Illeron's study. A statuesque man dressed in gold and silver stepped through the rip, which closed behind him. He was strikingly handsome, with strong bone structure and sharply observant eyes. The powerful essence surrounding him had nothing to do with the enormous gleaming sword in his right hand or the shadow of a glittering, sparkling crown across his brow.

"There was no need to come, your majesty," Illeron said from next to me, confirming my suspicion that the King of the Seelie court had just graced us with his presence.

"I beg to differ." The king glared in the direction of the pond. "I believe that is a siren, and considering the wound in the woman's shoulder, she has targeted your companion. They hunt by blood scent."

Before I could look in the direction, he indicated, an unearthly sound rent the air. A strange vibration began throbbing through me. It was as though my veins were resonating with the sound. Beginning almost pleasantly, it swiftly turned uncomfortable. Thrumming and then buzzing pulsed through me. The pain escalated swiftly until I realized someone was keening in pain. That someone was me. I was vaguely aware of a flurry of activity around me.

Standing, not wholly of my own accord, I stepped toward the siren. The pain eased slightly. I had a brief impression of an ugly bird-like woman dressed in weirdly floating gossamer layers. It was almost as though she was suspended in water, not air. Her golden eyes focused sharply on me, bloodlust making them glint.

"No!" Illeron planted himself in front of me, wrapping his arms around me and blocking any forward motion. Threading his hands through my hair, he guided my head so that his mesmerizing green eyes locked with mine.

"Don't move. Once you are in reach, she will kill you and eat you."

"We could transport her," Casimir suggested.

"It won't stop the siren," the king pointed out.

"We can attack the creature directly then," the unnamed shadow elf suggested.

The siren's song intensified again, ripping through me. Illeron's arms tightened, and his heels dug into the gravel pathway as he fought my unwilling efforts to move toward my doom. Determination flared in his eyes.

The king spoke. "The siren's spell won't be broken unless we attack her with a bronze blade covered in the victim's blood."

Illeron's eyes darkened. After firmly pressing his lips to my forehead, he called out to his brother. "Casimir, hold her."

"Why?" he demanded. "No foolishness."

"None," Illeron promised. "I have a bronze blade."

"But you have healed her. There isn't enough blood left, and you can't draw more. The binding will prevent it." Casimir's voice sounded uncannily calm.

"But you can," Illeron pointed out. "I will give you the blade."

I felt the tingle of Illeron's retrieval magic at the same time the siren's call intensified again. The throbbing was so intense that I couldn't hold back a cry of pain. The spell flung me against Illeron's embrace at the exact moment he loosened his hold to pluck the blade from the air.

Suddenly, I was running toward my death with a bevy of shouts at my back. I sobbed with the effort of trying to resist, but to no avail.

Illeron

I plucked the child's dagger that Avril had attempted to steal from its keeping place just as Avril tore from my grasp.

"Casimir," I called as I tossed the blade across the gap between us. Not even bothering to check to see if he caught it, I darted after Avril's stumbling form. She fought the call, contorting her body in a wild-eyed effort to slow her progress.

Casimir beat me to Avril by the barest of moments. Striking with frightful precision, he reopened her wound. Then he turned wraith. With the barest shadow of variation, he flew from dark corner to black shade across the garden to the siren's side. He plunged the dagger up into the siren's heart.

I reached Avril just as the siren's song ended in a prolonged shriek that made my ears ache. But I didn't care. Avril dropped into my arms, limp, sobbing, and very much alive. I buried my face in her hair and clung to her. It was a few moments before I recalled she was bleeding again and initialized healing.

"I couldn't stop." A harsh sob shook her narrow shoulders. "She was controlling my whole body."

"I know, love," I whispered, smoothing her wildly tumbled tresses from her face. "Hush, now. It is over. You are safe."

She shuddered. "I wish that were true."

"Lady Avril said a shadow elf attacked her." Favian, one of my most trusted veteran shadow elves, stood over us.

Avril nodded grimly. "I didn't see him well enough to recognize him, and his voice wasn't familiar, but it was definitely a shadow elf."

Unease filled me. My arms drew her closer, reassuring myself that she was safe, at least for the moment.

"Casimir, we need an accounting of every elf's whereabouts."

Favian and Casimir both disappeared.

Avril's favorite shawl was stained with blood and the shoulder of her tunic gapped. I made a note to replace them both immediately. The last thing she needed was a reminder of this night.

The Seelie king watched with obvious concern as I helped Avril to her feet. She wobbled like a newborn colt.

"Let me." He opened a portal into the study.

Avril's dark eyes widened in awe. "How do you do that?"

An amused smile crossed the usually reserved king's face. "It is a bit of inherited magic, you might say."

"Can all Seelie open…" She appeared to struggle with a word for what she was seeing.

"Open portals?" The king supplied. "No, I am one of the few."

"Why wasn't I allowed to meet him?" She asked me.

Despite the show of strength and attempt at normalcy with her friendly chatter, I could feel her body's warning signs of an imminent collapse. Even an elf would have struggled to remain upright after such a traumatic event.

"We feared you would be caught in the curse because you are human," I replied.

"Human female," the king clarified.

Then Avril stumbled. I took the opportunity to sweep her into my arms right before crossing the portal's edge. She sagged against me with a soft sigh, giving way to exhaustion. Striding to the chaise with the intention of laying her down, I found myself suddenly very hesitant to let her go. I stood there a moment, staring down at her delicate features.

"Shall we resume?" the king asked.

Reluctantly settling her on the chaise, I turned to face my guest. "My apologies for the interruption."

The king inclined his head with far more ease than I had observed since the beginning of our meeting. "Some things are of more immediate importance. Will she recover?"

I gazed down at Avril for a brief moment. Her shoulder was healing. There would be not even be a scar by the morning. For all of the trauma, I sensed only exhaustion. "She will likely be up and about within a day if I can hold her back that long."

"Why didn't the shadow elf kill her outright?"

I frowned. "I suspect to hide the fact there is a traitor in our midst. If we hadn't been so quick to respond, Avril would be dead from the siren, and we would only be reinforcing our security against sirens, not looking for a mole."

"But why her?" The Seelie's eyes narrowed. "Is there something special about her?"

I gazed down at Avril's prone form. An orphan, a thief, and my companion—unless there were some missions in her past that I hadn't been able to uncover, the only possible reason for the targeting was her association with me.

"Her connection to me." I brushed her hair with my hand, catching a loose curl with one finger. "How that leads to someone wanting her dead, is beyond me, though."

"Then perhaps we should reconvene another time after you have figured that out. A life is a precious thing, and worth your full attention." He had been eager to take every opportunity to cut our meeting short until Favian's call for help. I had been astonished when the king had followed me into the garden clearly intending to assist. It was strange behavior considering his off-putting approach all evening.

"No," I immediately protested. "As long as you don't mind discussing things in front of my companion, I would wish to continue."

Sadness moved across the king's features. "I fear, despite your kind offer earlier, there is little you can do to free me from the constraints that have been forced upon me." His gaze fell upon Avril's sleeping form. "My opponent has chosen a ruthless set of demands in exchange for my freedom. Demands I am debating whether or not to even attempt."

"There is no other way to break—" I hesitated to say the word curse.

The king stopped me himself. "I cannot speak to the particulars of my release lest it make my struggle to fulfill them easier. I can say, if all humans are as brave as your companion, I have hope."

Multiple questions jumped to mind, but not all of them were constructive. I pressed my lips together, resisting letting them loose. Discussing the curse would only drive the king away because of the geas put upon him.

"Until that time, then, you can do nothing about the wild hunt?"

"I am very limited in my power concerning this, but I can promise to do all I can to move it to safer regions."

"Understood." I bowed to him. "Thank you for the effort."

"Of course." He inclined his head to me. "And should there be anything within my ability, do contact me. I can promise to listen."

"Thank you, your majesty." I bowed again as he opened a portal to his realm.

"Thank you, Spymaster Whispier." Then he stepped through the portal and was gone.

TWELVE

Avril

The next morning when I woke, I was surprised to find I wasn't sleeping in my bed. Wrapped in something soft and warm, I was pleasantly comfortable and reluctant to move. Slowly, my senses woke to other stimuli. Watching the light and shadows playing across the honeycombed ceiling of Illeron's study, I ran through my memories of the night before. No matter how I tried to recall the face or any identifying details about the elf that attacked me, I kept coming up empty. I hadn't seen him.

The familiar softness of my shawl against my cheek no longer felt reassuring. Shadow elves moved silently through the palace constantly. Flickering from shadow to shadow, any of them could be the assassin. A shiver shook me. Something tightened around my knee. Illeron sat on the floor at the side of the chaise. His dark head rested on the edge, and one elegant hand was curled around my knee as though to ensure I didn't disappear while he slept.

Someone, a shadow elf by the sound, moved through a shadow near the window. They didn't stay, just flitted in and promptly out again as though to check I was still there and left.

Strangely, I took comfort in Illeron's presence. Surely, the elf out to kill me wouldn't dare do it while Illeron was present, even if he was asleep. I tried to relax. Illeron's soft respirations and his subtle scent were reassuring in many ways.

I rested my head back against the couch's plump cushions. Memories of being held in his arms the night before as he physically restrained me from answering the siren's call brought a warm flush to my cheeks. Only a few months ago, I had never encountered an elf. I had just thought of them as manipulative and scheming. Now I owed their most powerful spymaster my life many times over. I groaned softly. If I survived this, how would I ever repay him?

The hand around my knee tightened again as Illeron's head stirred.

"Morning," I whispered.

He lifted his face and regarded me with slightly unfocused eyes. "Avril." His husky voice made my stomach flutter. "How are you feeling?"

"Well, thanks to you."

He squeezed my knee gently before standing. I expected him to move away, but instead, he sat on the edge of the chaise. "Have you tried sitting up?"

"No."

"Come." He caught my upper arm and eased me into a sitting position, turning me so he could examine my shoulder. His fingers probed the place where the knife had scored my skin the night before. "Does this hurt?"

I shook my head. "Any scar?"

"None." He leaned back so he could study my features. "And the rest of you? Anything hurt? How do you feel?"

"Only scared," I admitted. "I am not exactly equipped to fend off a shadow elf."

Gathering me against him, he pressed a kiss to my temple before whispering in my ear. "Then trust me to handle that part."

I burrowed deeper into his embrace and tried to rest in the fact that he was promising to protect me. It helped some. Still, he was only one elf and limited in his skill set.

"Casimir and I came up with a plan last night. He has some theories as to our traitor-assassin." He squeezed gently before retreating. "Don't worry." Smoothing my hair back from my face, he caressed my cheek. "I won't leave you until we catch him."

"Thank you," I whispered. "I don't know what I would do if—"

"We will stop him. I will keep you safe." The resolution in his expression gave me a small measure of reassurance. He would do everything he could to keep me safe, but he wasn't infallible. Before I could put this into words though, he was pulling me to my feet. "You will feel better after cleaning up and eating some food."

He escorted me to my bedchamber. After searching the whole room and setting a spell on the floor, he left while I dressed.

In one way, he was correct. I did feel marginally better after washing up and donning new clothing. However, the sight of my blood-stained shawl resting on the end of the bed made me hesitate. My situation could change in an instant.

I opened the door to find Illeron leaning against the wall beside it. His curls were damp, and he wore an emerald tunic over leather leggings instead of the formal gray from last night. He wordlessly fell into step next to me as I walked toward the kitchen.

"I have a meeting with Casimir in an hour. Will that be enough time for you to eat breakfast?" he asked as we approached the kitchen door.

"Easily."

"Good." He led the way into the bright and airy kitchen. "Waldorf! What is for breakfast?"

The brownie didn't even flinch in surprise at his master's loud greeting. "Scrambled chicken eggs, bacon, and melon slices are already prepared. Do you have any additional requests?"

"Toast and tea would be wonderful." Illeron settled on a stool at the counter and motioned for me to join him. "With haste, if possible. We have a strategy meeting approaching."

"Of course." Waldorf slid a warm plate across the counter with a wink.

"How is your family, Waldorf?" Illeron asked with friendly eagerness as he set to consuming the eggs. "Your daughter still studying under Master Jerroth?"

"She is! Her skill in silverwork has improved so swiftly that Master Jerroth sent a request to me that I allow her to contract in his workshop as a journeyman." The brownie glowed with parental pride.

"How many children do you have?" I asked. I was ashamed that I hadn't thought to ask Waldorf about his family.

"Five, four sons and a daughter." Waldorf's smile dimmed slightly. "The wife wanted more, but it wasn't to be."

"Melyn is their youngest." Illeron volunteered before taking another bite.

Waldorf's grin widened again. "She is our delight. Each of our children is special to us, but she is our only daughter and unique."

"And gifted." Illeron waved a fork at his cook. "You should bring in something to show Avril." He turned to me. "The delicacy of the work she produces is breathtaking. I am planning on commissioning a new front gate from her as soon as she begins accepting projects."

"Truly?" Waldorf regarded his employer in wonder.

"There is no rush, though." The elf assured the brownie. "The gate will hold for years to come. Let her enjoy her learning years. The gate can wait until she is confident in her abilities and her skills match her talents."

"Thank you, Master Whispier. But can I mention it to Melyn? She would be delighted to know that she already has someone interested in hiring her once she completes her studies."

"Certainly." Illeron scraped his plate clean. "Now, if only one of your sons was as talented with food as you are."

"Tortian completed his training four weeks ago," Waldorf protested. "He cooks nearly as well as me."

"Nearly?" Illeron's eyebrows rose in mock horror. "I hope he doesn't kill the lot of us at next month's banquet."

Waldorf's sputtering brought a reluctant smile to my lips. The two of them bantered for a bit as I finished my own meal. It was good to see I wasn't the only one who would tease the brownie, or the self-contained spymaster, for that matter. Witnessing the rapport between the two of them warmed my heart. Illeron need to be teased.

My chest ached at the thought of not being Illeron's companion, but anyone could see that this couldn't last. As much as I wished to remain connected like this forever, enjoying Illeron's constant company, I knew I couldn't. I was an outsider.

Unlike these seemingly immortal beings, I would age. I doubted Illeron would enjoy my presence once my limited beauty faded. Sure, he enjoyed kissing me and holding me now. He liked the way I looked. That wouldn't last.

"You have grown quiet," Illeron observed, drawing me back to the present. "Does anything hurt?"

"Did the food grow cold?" Waldorf asked. "I can heat it up. Do you want anything else? I can make more toast. Tea?"

I shook my head. "I just lost my appetite." I offered him a warm smile. "The food tasted delicious."

The two males exchanged a glance.

I groaned. "No reading into it. I am fine. My stomach is just full." It was the truth.

"Good," Illeron stood and offered me his open hand.

Instinctively, I put mine in his but instantly regretted it. He took the opportunity to use our joined hands to pull me close, tucking my arm against his side and pinning it there with his arm.

"Thank you, Waldorf," he called over his shoulder as he almost dragged me out of the kitchen and down the corridor toward the gymnasium or, as I had heard it referred to occasionally, the training room.

"I have something to show you." His step was light and quick. In his eagerness, he appeared to forget our height difference. His longer legs quickly ate up the distance, and I had to hurry to keep up.

"What is it?"

"I have been thinking how you could defend yourself against a shadow elf, and I have some ideas." After that, he wouldn't disclose any more until we reached the center of the gymnasium.

Morning sunlight flooded the space. The warmth seemed to sink into my bones, and I relaxed slightly. The few shadows were pale, which meant I could see any wraithwalkers lingering in them if I happened to be looking in their direction. Also, the patches of sunlight were bright, which I understood hindered shadow elves' abilities.

As though reading my mind, Illeron said, "Shadow elves are slowed by direct sunlight. It hampers their wraithwalking abilities and hinders their use of their natural magic. However, these windows won't help you much in a close combat fight."

I frowned up at him. "Why? I am not completely helpless."

An amused lightening of his eyes was my only warning before he snapped his fingers. The room instantly cloaked in darkness as though someone had turned off the sun. I felt the air move as he passed. Then, he was standing behind me. The firm pressure of his hand encircling my middle over my tunic was there and gone before I could even attempt to jump away. Then, as I turned to confront him, he had returned to his previous position and snapped his fingers again. The sunlight returned. Only the slight disarray of his clothing betrayed that he had moved.

"Direct sunlight only slows a shadow elf to the speed of a light elf at night and vice versa." He produced a delicate silver lattice pendant encasing a glowing emerald. The chain attached was just as elegantly simple and graceful as the slender swirling twists of silver entwined around the brilliant stone. "A spell," he explained as I admired the pendant. "It is embedded in the stone."

"But won't he sense it?" I asked.

"That is the beauty of it," he said as he started undoing the clasp. "The spell is a simple one, no more powerful than the ones on your brownie-spelled cloak. But it will pack a powerful punch when you utter the trigger word."

"What does it do?"

He moved around behind me to clasp the delicate chain around my neck. "I will show you."

"Surely it isn't strong enough to stop a shadow elf if it can feel like a brownie spell." I moved my hair aside so it wouldn't tangle in the necklace. The pendant settled against my skin, cool and slightly tingling. As my skin warmed the metal, the tingling disappeared. Instead, I became very aware of Illeron's hands resting against the back of my neck as he lingered behind me.

"It has multiple purposes." He stepped back away from me. "The trigger word is my name spoken in a low tone."

"Illeron?"

A blinding light flared to life. I closed my eyes in an effort not to lose my sight, but I was a hair too late. Splotches danced behind my closed eyelids. A pressure pulsed out from my chest, cocooning me.

The air in the room shifted.

"You summoned?" Casimir's calm voice announced his arrival.

"Can you penetrate it?" Illeron asked.

A heavy silence followed for a moment. "What is it?"

"A spell of my own devising."

"I see the summoning element."

"Linked to me."

Casimir's soft snort came from behind me. A second later, his voice spoke from my left. "You should link it to me as well. We both know you won't reach her in time, but I might."

"Adding you would be tricky. As it is, everything in the spell is delicately balanced."

"The light, the summoning…" Casimir's voice faded to quiet as though he were focusing. "…a personal protection spell against weapons?" His surprise made me want to open my eyes, but I suspected I would be blinded. The shadow elf was so rarely surprised. "It is easily bypassed."

"Humor me."

A grunt and something passed before my face, momentarily blocking the light. Then Casimir's hands settled around my throat, loose and non-threatening but startling all the same. Reflexes kicked in. I bent and twisted, freeing myself from his grip. Blindly, I punched up into where a human's abdomen would be. He evaded it with ease, grabbing my wrist and twisting it up behind my back. I slipped free, but I could tell Casimir wasn't really trying. There was no real strength in his grasp. He didn't attempt to grab me again.

"How do I stop the spell?" I demanded.

"Repeat the trigger word."

I whispered his name, and suddenly the light disappeared. I gratefully opened my eyes only to frown at the sight of the brothers glaring at each other.

"It is basically useless," Casimir pointed out. "The anti-blade limits the attacker, but a shadow elf will have no problem subduing or killing her with just their hands. Also, it blinds her. The light is hardly limiting when the assailant has already appeared."

Illeron grimaced. "I will remove the light."

"And add me to the summons?"

"Yes."

Casimir turned to assess me. "She is feisty. I am not sure her assailant will expect that, but he might move so fast she never has a chance. All we can do is hope that he needs something from her and thus won't kill her outright."

My stomach twisted. Not exactly the news I wanted to hear.

"Then it is a good thing this is only a tiny part of my plan. We will make it so that he doesn't have the opportunity to touch her." Illeron's eyes darkened ominously. "We know he isn't working alone, whoever he is. Someone has hired him, and we have a lead on whom."

"I also have some possible leads regarding his identity," Casimir added.

"When will they be available for questioning?"

Casimir eyed his brother. "Two will be in your study this afternoon. The third, and most likely one, will be arriving tomorrow morning."

"And none of them suspect."

"They think they are being given an exclusive assignment."

Illeron nodded.

Casimir glared at his brother and bowed to me before stepping into a shadow and disappearing.

"He seemed disgruntled," I commented.

"Casimir?" Illeron distractedly glanced at me as he strode off toward the end of the gymnasium. "He is always like that."

"No, he seemed more so than usual."

"Probably because I woke him from sleep when I summoned him."

I groaned. "Please don't antagonize your brother on my account. He already doesn't like me."

Illeron paused with two mock daggers in one hand and a scarf in the other. "What do you mean? Casimir likes you." Genuine surprise written across his face undermined my first impression that he was joking.

"Truly?"

"Avril, he requested to be added to the summons on the spell."

"Insisted on it actually," I admitted. "Still, he…" How to say it without being offensive.

"He has always struggled with showing affection." Illeron approached and offered me a mock dagger. "Trust me, he likes you. If not, he would have never agreed to be added to the summons."

"I figured he was insisting for your sake since you are attached to me."

Illeron's eyes flared silver in mossy green darkness. "I would say I am a bit more than attached."

Avoiding that intensity, I focused back on the previous issue. "When we first made our agreement, your brother was clearly angry about it. What has changed?"

Illeron sighed. "Our father took a companion after our mother died. It filled at least some of the void left by her death."

"He married her?" I had never heard of an elf marrying a human.

"It wasn't a true elven marriage. Just a human one."

"There is a difference?"

"One is a melding of life forces, and the other only an exchange of vows." He studied my features with an expression close to longing before abruptly shifting his attention to his weapons. He tossed the dagger into the air and caught it. "Regardless, Casimir struggled with our father's distance after our mother's death. Taking a companion didn't fill the void for our father. And when the woman died, all three of us fell into grieving yet again."

He eyed me from beneath lowered brows. "When we made our agreement, Casimir saw it as the first step toward pain and loss. Hence the annoyance at my foolishness for lowering my defenses. But risk is a price one must pay to live."

"Basically, he was just acting like a protective big brother."

"Little brother," he corrected with a smirk. "I am the elder."

I laughed and turned my focus to examining the rubber weapon he had handed me. "What is this for?"

"Practice." He retreated a few steps. "I am going to attack you, and you are going to fend me off."

"I don't think—"

He lunged at me so fast that I barely got my knife up to stop him. Looming over me with a menacing glint in his eye, he smiled. "Don't think. React."

THIRTEEN

Illeron

Bounding backward away from me, Avril adjusted the grip on her knife and fell into a ready stance. I advanced, feinting to her left. She easily blocked it. Keeping my speed down, I tested her skills and reaction times. Her responses were instinctive and quick, a sign of being well trained. However, she wasn't fast enough to fend off an elf.

Using more force than I should've, I struck her knife from her hand. We broke apart. She retreated, breathing heavily from the exertion. A glimmer of frustration flared in her expression before she suppressed it.

"You aren't even breathing heavily," she accused.

"Your reflexes are good."

She shook her head as she leaned forward in an attempt to catch her breath. "Don't hesitate. Just say it." Peering up through the strands of hair that had escaped from her braid, she grimaced. "It is hopeless."

"Not entirely," I countered. "You have a character quality that he won't expect."

"What? The ability to annoy you?"

I allowed a wry smile as I plucked the errant blade from the floor. "The element of the unexpected."

She blinked up at me with a frown.

"You constantly surprise me by doing what I least expect. Here," I offered her back her knife. "Come at me again. This time don't think about your training. Do something unexpected. Set me off balance."

Surprisingly, she did. Charging me with a wild yell, she tackled me around the middle. I stepped back in surprise. Before I could get my bearings, she had jabbed her knife at an angle that would have jabbed up and under my ribs, a killing blow if it had been long enough to reach my heart.

I grabbed her wrist. She twisted away, dropping the knife into her free hand and slashing at my side as she turned. I released her, only to kick out at her legs. She fell but immediately rolled to her feet again. Knife still in hand, she lunged at me, but at the last moment, she swerved. Ducking beneath my arm, she landed another blow to my ribs.

"You are purposefully moving slowly," she accused.

"I am, but partially since I am pleasantly surprised."

"Stop it." Anger sparked in her eyes as she tightened her grip on the mock weapon. "I can't train if you aren't trying."

"I don't want to hurt you."

She grimaced. "He is going to do more than hurt me. He intends to kill me."

Conceding her point, I increased my aggression. After a handful of instant pins, she began to grow frustrated. When I pinned her to the floor a sixth time, this time with my face inches from hers as I knelt over her, she got a mischievous glint in her eye. Pulling her hand free from my relaxing grip, she reached up and threaded her fingers through my curls. Then, she kissed me.

I pulled back, stunned. "What was that for?"

She laughed. "You said to be impulsive."

"I didn't say to kiss him."

"He wasn't the one I was kissing." She studied my face. "Now, I have offended you."

"Not offended." The twisted pain in my chest wasn't offense. It was a strange mixture of fear and desire. I groaned.

Never had she been more appealing with her hair wild and spread out around her head and her dark eyes sparkling with amusement. Add to that the lingering impression of her mouth on mine, and I had to close my eyes to resist claiming her mouth in return.

I buried my face in her shoulder. I had promised I would wait before declaring myself. Waiting until she was free to say no without fearing I would throw her out to the mercies of the elf intent on killing her. I rolled to the side, landing hard on my back. The pain helped to cool the ardor pumping through my veins.

She shifted. Fingers traced my ear, smoothing back the curls that always rioted over their points. "Illeron?"

"Give me a moment, love."

She didn't retreat. Instead, she moved closer. Cool fingertips smoothed my forehead, tracing my eyebrows.

"Did I hurt you?" she asked hesitantly.

"No." I drew in a deep breath. She smelled of oranges and cinnamon.

"Then what is wrong?" She caressed my cheek.

It took everything in me not to lean into her hand and savor the sensation of her touch.

"There." She smoothed the crease between my brows. "You are in pain."

"I am." I groaned. "I am dying at the thought of losing you."

She went still and silent for a moment.

"I am not going anywhere. Not willingly anyway."

I grimaced. "I know." I opened my eyes and turned my head to meet her worried gaze. I had to change the topic, or I would confess something I couldn't voice yet. "No kissing the villain."

She rolled her eyes. "I wouldn't."

"Then what was the kiss for?"

"To make a point." She sat up.

"What point?" I sat up as well, turning to face her.

"If I can kiss you, I can bite his nose."

I laughed. "You were thinking about him while you were kissing me?"

"No." Her smirk disappeared. "I was thinking about you, but the point stands."

I conceded the point.

No amount of drilling was going to make it so she could fend off an elven attacker. I resisted admitting it, though. We agreed to be done for the day and cleaned up. But I resolved that we would be back at it again on the morrow and every day thereafter. I wanted her as equipped as possible. In the meantime, I intended to never let her leave my sight.

Avril

Illeron worked like a man obsessed. Reading, hearing, and processing reports filled the hours and nearly crowded out lunch. Only when everything had been cleared did he agree to interview assistant candidates.

We were three interviews in when suddenly Casimir stood in the shadows of the corner. Illeron didn't indicate he noticed him. Instead, he simply continued the interview.

"What qualifications did you bring?" Illeron asked the light elf standing across from him. I had caught this one's name, Chislon

"I am skilled in processing copious amounts of information quickly and efficiently. My previous employer commended me on my organizational skills regularly."

"Who is your character reference?"

The light elf hesitated. I lowered my book and watched with interest. Every candidate so far had eagerly announced their character references.

"Do you have one?" Illeron asked.

"I do. It is Elite Commander Corbin."

Illeron's eyebrows rose. "The Night Crow?"

Casimir stirred in the shadows.

The candidate nodded, his attention split between Illeron and Casimir. "I served as his military liaison for a year while he was between assistants. I also functioned as his personal secretary before that."

"So, why the hesitation?"

"He is my uncle."

"Then you wish to stand on your own reputation and find your own way?"

"More that people assume I have influence over my uncle, or I have access to his secrets." Chislon grimaced. "Or they fear my connection to him. He doesn't exactly have a reputation for letting those who insult his family walk away without consequences."

Illeron nodded. "True. Do you have an issue with keeping secrets from him?"

"No. I am my own elf."

Illeron studied Chislon for a few moments, letting the silence fill the room. Unlike the previous candidates, he waited without fidgeting or any signs of discomfort.

"I will take you on as a trial. The position comes with room and board. I expect you to be available as needed. The pay will be commensurate according to the level of effort. I will expect you to learn on the job. Do you have any questions or concerns?"

"I would wish to live somewhere else."

Illeron eyed him with interest. "How much of a delay from summoning to appearing should I expect?"

"Twenty minutes." Chislon tilted his head. "How often should I expect summons at odd hours?"

"Hard to say. We ordinarily don't, but when we do, I will need an immediate response."

"Understood."

Illeron lifted his eyebrows at the younger elf. "Are you still interested in the position?"

"Definitely."

"In that case, you are hired for a probationary term to see if we suit." Illeron motioned toward the door into the corridor. "My house manager, Ergon, will show you around. I will expect you back here within a half-hour for an explanation of your duties."

"Thank you, Lord Spymaster." Chislon bowed perfunctorily in Illeron's direction and offered both Casimir and me a respectful nod. Then he departed through the door with admirable directness.

"I like him," I declared.

"What news do you bring?" Illeron asked Casimir.

"We figured out who was behind the attack. Loriena has been seen mingling with some of our shadow elves. One of them came forward, saying that she offered him money for information. He declined, but he suspects she has approached other elves." Casimir grimaced. "It would explain how the siren slipped through the wards. All it takes is for one of our guards to cooperate."

"Any progress on narrowing that possible traitor down?" Illeron began pulling reports from the air.

"We have it narrowed down to three. I will be interviewing two of them in your study today." Dark smudges marred the skin beneath Casimir's eyes, and exhaustion glazed his eyes.

"When did you last sleep?" I asked him.

He shrugged with one shoulder. "Two nights ago."

Illeron straightened. "Go sleep."

"But the first interview is scheduled in an hour."

"Do you have anyone you trust?"

"Keir," Casimir rubbed the side of his face. "I suppose I could have him do it."

"Let him. Go get some rest. You are no use to any of us half asleep."

Casimir nodded wearily. With a soft whoosh of air, he was gone.

"Is this normal?" I asked.

Illeron was already examining a new map. "What?"

"Dead on his feet. Lacking sleep."

"He struggles with sleeping at times of high stress." Illeron paused and glanced at me over the top of the map, green eyes darkening. "I didn't notice this time. Thank you for pointing it out."

"I am sorry that I am causing such difficulty."

Illeron dropped his map. It missed the table's edge and fell to the floor. He ignored it, stalking around the table to stand above me. He pulled my chair around to face him so that I had to crane my neck to meet his dark gaze beneath his lowered brows. "What do you mean by that?"

"You are going through so much effort to protect me. I am sorry to be the cause of all the hassle."

He began shaking his head before I had even finished my apology. "There is nothing to apologize for. We have discovered a leak in my network that I had no inkling existed. I owe you because of this, not the other way around."

"But you are working so hard to keep me alive."

"Life is precious." The silver in his gaze flared briefly. "Yours is doubly so. This is no hassle." He knelt before me so I no longer had to crane my neck. "No foolish sacrifices."

I nodded. "I am not planning any."

"Good." He leaned in, grazing my cheek with a breath-like kiss before withdrawing.

"Master Whispier?" Chislon had returned.

As Illeron turned to begin training his new assistant, I picked up my book from my lap. But I didn't read. My thoughts were too full already.

FOURTEEN

Avril

A week passed. Chislon settled in and quickly grew comfortable enough to argue with Illeron, which I saw as a good sign. The two elves would discuss the reports, debate the possible meanings, and compile lists of actions that needed to be taken. I spent hours listening to them.

"The woodwose will be decimated!" Chislon protested. "The warlords are better armed and better prepared."

"Are you sure about that?" Illeron demanded as he threw himself into his chair with a self-assured air. He glanced over at me. I lowered my eyes to my book again, but my ears were tuned into the argument.

"Yes! The woodwose are peaceful. Most of them are healers, farmers, and craftsmen—not warriors."

"That is where you are wrong. All of them are trained to fight from an early age. They learned centuries ago that their peaceful reputation makes them a target." Illeron picked up an eraser from the table and began fingering it.

"That doesn't mean we shouldn't warn them," Chislon protested.

"I did, weeks ago."

"Or try to stop the warlords from attacking."

"Ah!" Illeron flung the eraser across the room, so it bounced off the wall. "Now there is the rub."

Chislon stared at him in complete confusion. "What?"

"What can we do to stop the warlords from attacking the woodwose?"

"Negotiation?"

"I tried that. The warlords want their land and resources and refuse to discuss anything less than a full surrender of all of it."

"Political persuasion."

Illeron snorted. "We have none. These particular warlords answer to no one and believe that they depend on no one."

"Force?" Chislon asked hesitantly.

"Are you proposing we declare war on the two warlords to stop them from inciting conflict with the woodwose?"

"That wouldn't make sense." Chislon ran a hand through his hair, standing the pale straight strands on end.

"Which is my whole point. For now, I am planning on recommending we watch, wait, and support the woodwose as best we can. Now is not the time to step in. However —" Illeron raised a hand to cut off Chislon's efforts to retort. "However, I am not saying we don't take decisive action later when we can affect greater change in the situation than now."

Chislon pulled his mouth tight, obviously resisting the temptation to disagree. But when Illeron assigned him the task of writing the recommendation out, he worked just as swiftly and efficiently as usual.

The two of them were debating the exact wording when one of the Seelie King's gates opened in the middle of the study. But instead of the Seelie King, someone much smaller stepped through the light effused opening. The woman only came to Illeron's waist when he stood to his feet to greet her. Her brown skin glowed with health. Dressed all in green and covered in ivy, including a growth of moss in her hair, she had an otherworld appearance. I had never met one of her kind before.

Illeron bowed to her. "Mistress Mingina, to what do I owe the pleasure."

"No pleasure." She produced a piece of bark from beneath her ivy-covered clothing. "King requests your presence immediately."

"Now?"

"I said immediately, didn't I?" She scanned the room and spotted me. "Didn't I?" she asked me.

"You did."

"Then we will come with haste. Let me—"

Chislon was already disappearing documents from the table.

The Mistress Mingina's features tightened into a scowl of displeasure. "Now!"

"Odon!" Illeron called.

The shadow elf stepped out of the shadow behind the drapes and bowed.

"Protect her with your life," Illeron ordered as he adjusted the magic around the edges of the room. I could feel the wards tightening around the palace and especially on the perimeter of the study. "Avril?"

"Yes?" I stood. "Can't I go with you?"

"Humans can't walk the paths of the Seelie without being altered forever." He drew close, settling his hands on my shoulders. "I dare not take you with me. Odon will protect you until I return." He rested his forehead against mine with his eyes closed. "Don't do anything foolish," he whispered.

"I won't. Well not intentionally, that is."

He laughed softly, kissed my forehead, and then left, calling for Chislon to follow him. The three of them disappeared through the portal. Then with a sharp snap, the room was suddenly very empty.

"Shall we go find lunch?" I asked my keeper.

Odon smiled warmly. "Lead the way."

Illeron

Mistress Mingina glared at my new assistant as we prepared to exit the Seelie Realm after meeting with the king. The whole realm resonated with the occupants' grief. Their king was compelled to ride in the Wild Hunt until he could find a way to break the curse.

"Please assure the Seelie King we will do all we can to research his curse. There must be a way to break it. By their nature, curses are meant to be broken."

Mistress Mingina pursed her lips. "As you have said before." Her dark eyes flashed as she glanced at Chislon. "However, not all elves are trustworthy."

Chislon started to open his mouth, but I forestalled him. "Thank you again for your hospitality." I bowed to her, motioning for Chislon to head through the portal before me. I didn't trust Mistress Mingina not to close it on my assistant before he was all the way through.

Thankfully, Chislon followed my prompting, but not without a slightly petulant glance over his shoulder.

The moment I stepped through the portal into my palace's entry hall, I knew something was wrong.

"I didn't know I wasn't supposed to touch the vase," Chislon protested the moment the portal closed behind us. "How was I supposed to know my touch would contaminate it?"

"Hush." I cut him off with an angry wave. "I need to concentrate."

The wards on the palace were secure. I reached out toward my study. The perimeter still glowed with the intact ward, but I couldn't sense the spelled necklace, which meant it wasn't around Avril's neck.

"The assassin has Avril." Anger boiled in my gut. If he hurt her— I slid my fighting swords from their storage spell. The familiar weight of them calmed me slightly. "Also, Loriena is here."

"How do you know?" Chislon asked as he drew closer. He produced a short sword forged from dragon steel, a black metal strong enough to slice through most other weapons.

"Someone has Avril," I insisted. "Her personal ward isn't active, and I sense four people, one of whom is Loriena, in my study. There should only be two at most."

"But the others could be anyone," Chislon pointed out.

I scanned the room. A tingling at the back of my head kept my guard up. Then I spotted it. A telltale shimmer coated the first three steps of the staircase to the second floor. I crouched and examined the spell work. Definitely shadow elf made. I motioned for Chislon to take my place and look as well.

"A warning spell," my assistant whispered.

I set my blades soundlessly on the foyer table before slipping free of my restrictive coat and casting it aside. Rolling up my shirt sleeves, I adjusted the shirt's fit over my shoulders, loosening it. Freedom of movement could make me a hairbreadth faster, which could mean the difference between Avril's life and her death.

"We fight?" Chislon asked as he quickly followed my lead.

"If we must." Part of me wished I could just kill the assailant outright, but I couldn't. Too many questions remained, and I needed Loriena compliant.

"What is the plan?"

"Get Avril back. I don't share."

"Very well." My assistant rolled his shoulders and headed toward the stairs.

I cut him off with an arm. "Without triggering the warning spell."

He nodded his understanding. Leaping with ease over the spelled stairs, he landed silently one stair above them. I followed. Then, we stalked up the stairs together.

We switched places upon reaching the study door, so I took the lead, hiding my swords behind my left leg. I opened the door with my right hand.

Light streamed through the far windows, outlining the dark form of a copper-skinned elf. In his shadow knelt Avril. One of the elf's dark hands gripped her pale throat. The sun glinted off the edge of a long thin knife in his other hand. Behind them, Loriena paced, tossing a bottle from hand to hand.

"When are they coming back?" she demanded.

"Unknown," Lynan replied. "I think you should poison her now and be done with it. Leave her carcass for him to find."

"No," Loriena held the bottle up to the light, admiring it. "I want him to watch her die."

I forced myself to glance around the room, locating the still form of Odon lying in his own blood. He still lived. As I intuitively knew the location of every shadow elf in my service, I knew he lived. Yet, he wouldn't for long if I didn't summon help, which I did. Casimir still slept, but my summons brought him to his feet. Assured he would appear within minutes, I turned my attention to the elf in the center of the room.

"Lynan?"

The shadow elf straightened. "Move, and she dies." His fingers around Avril's throat constricted as he brought his knife to rest against the underside of her jaw. Avril's eyes closed as she visibly fought panic. Only the shallow rise and fall of her chest still indicated that she lived.

"Hello, cousin." Loriena's voice dripped malice as she grinned at me. Bottle gone from her hands, she flashed her metallic claw fittings over her fingertips instead. "I heard you left your pet alone and came to keep her company."

Slipping my swords into hiding, I raised both of my hands. "I am unarmed."

"Don't move closer." Lynan's gaze flicked between me and the doorway. "Do it, Loriena. Then we can leave."

My cousin snorted. "Why hurry?" She flicked the nail covers again, and this time fluid sprayed the floor.

"What do you seek?" I asked.

She laughed bitterly. "Revenge. You took from me, and now I will take from you." She turned to Lynan, "Lift her chin."

The knife pressed against her skin. A trickle of blood dripped from the tip.

"Strange," Loriena muttered.

"What is strange?" I asked. Casimir was coming. I could feel him moving toward us. I just had to keep the mad elf talking.

Avril swallowed. Each breath I took ached. Just one slip, and she would die.

"How vulnerable humans are. Weak and stupid, they aren't worth the air they breathe. You have never had a human pet before. What is so special about this one?" Loriena grabbed a handful of Avril's hair and yanked her head back. The shadow elf scrambled to move out of the way of Loriena's poisoned fingers, but he didn't move fast enough. She hissed at him before caressing Avril's jaw.

Avril whimpered. I took an involuntary step toward her, but then Loriena rested the sharp metal tips against Avril's throat. "Stay there or I claw her throat now!"

"I love her." A sharp sensation in my chest dulled into an ache. "I love her and can't bear to be away from her."

"Fool!" Loriena hissed.

At that moment, Casimir arrived. A dark shadow of vengeance, he tore through the room, knocking the Loriena away from Avril, twisting our cousin's hand around so that the claw hovered inches from her own face. I dove for Lynan, driving him into the far wall. The satisfying crack of something breaking was my only reward, though. Lynan disappeared into a shadow before I could do anything more.

Avril collapsed forward, and I dove to catch her. Pulling her against me, I slipped my hand around her neck, tracing her jaw as I spread a healing spell over her skin. The nick from the knife beneath her jaw closed over almost instantly. Her pulse fluttered against my fingertips.

"Illeron?" she whispered hoarsely as she burrowed against me.

"I am here. She can't hurt you anymore."

"Can I kill her?" Casimir asked. His sleep-mussed hair gave him a half-crazed appearance as he dangled Loriena by the throat, a binding spell clamping the prisoner's arms to her side. The claws she had attempted to poison Avril with lay scattered on the rug at my brother's feet.

"It depends." I glanced over where my new assistant knelt next to Odon's prone form. "How is Odon?"

Avril lifted her head from my chest as she craned to see where her bodyguard had fallen.

"He is in pain, but he will live," Chislon reported.

"Then no death." Casimir's eyes lightened and widened as a nasty grin crossed his face. "But I can make you wish you were dead." Suddenly, they were no longer there. Loriena's scream echoed through the grounds before cutting off abruptly.

Chislon helped Odon to his feet. "Where might we find a healer?"

"Waldorf is our best healer on the premises at the moment. If the damage is too extensive, he can send for another."

Odon nodded. Then the two of them walked into the closest shadow and disappeared. Only Avril and I remained.

Avril leaned more heavily against me, her forehead touching my shoulder. "Is Odon really going to recover? Lynan hurt him badly. So much blood and…" She took a deep breath. "I am sorry. Lynan took my necklace, ripped it from my neck, and laughed that such a thing was supposed to protect me."

"It was meant to be a warning bell, a way for you to summon help."

"I know." She closed her eyes and sighed softly. "Did you mean what you said?"

It took me a moment to follow her chaotic thought pattern. "About loving you?"

She leaned back to study my features. "I know you only said it to keep your cousin talking—"

I kissed her. Pouring all my feelings into that one gesture, I drowned in the sensation of her responsive mouth on mine. Some moments later, we drew apart, but only far enough to catch our breath. She immediately hid her face against my shoulder.

"Does that answer your question?" I asked as I struggled to slow my galloping heart. Smoothing the curve of her back with the palm of my hand, I drank in the trace of orange in her hair and the pleasant weight of her leaning against me.

"But I am a human," she whispered.

"And I am an elf. What does that have to do with it?"

She laughed softly. "According to everyone, that means everything."

"It doesn't to me." I squeezed her gently. "Does it matter to you?"

"Not particularly."

"Stay with me, forever." I forced the words past the sudden tightness in my throat. "Marry me."

She grew still in my arms. I held my breath, chastising myself for my timing. I should've waited. She needed more time. Proposing immediately after a traumatic—

"Yes."

I couldn't believe my ears. "Are you certain?"

She laughed. "I wouldn't have said it if I wasn't."

I lifted her up and swung her around until she begged me to stop. Setting her on her feet again, I threaded my fingers through her hair, cradling her precious face between my palms. "I love you." Then, I kissed her.

EPILOGUE

Avril

The house was abuzz with activity. Our wedding was scheduled to happen in three days, and the preparations were in full swing. Casimir stood stiffly at attention in the center of the conservatory for a solid minute. Only his eyes moved to watch my progress as I watered the plants around the perimeter of the room. Finally, he spoke. "I won't be here for the wedding."

I paused in the middle of adjusting a fall of ivy that was encroaching on a nearby palm. Eyeing my future brother-in-law, I considered his statement. With Casimir, not everything was said explicitly.

"So, you have changed your mind, and no longer approve of our marrying?"

His brows lowered. "No. I approve."

"Then you don't agree with his insistence on a full elven ceremony."

"If he loves you enough to accept the inevitable survivor's grief, that is his choice." The slight tightening of his mouth was the only external sign of his irritation.

I hadn't gotten up the nerve to throw things at the tightly controlled shadow elf, but that didn't mean I wasn't going to provoke him in other ways. "I give up. Why aren't you going to be at the wedding?"

"I am leaving on a mission that I project will take a few weeks."

"Ah, which means you will miss the wedding."

"Precisely." He turned as though to leave.

"What is so important that it cannot wait?" I couldn't see Illeron assigning him a task that would conflict with witnessing our vow exchange. "Does Illeron know about the mission?"

"He knows I won't be present."

I frowned as I turned to study him. Crossing my arms, I glared. "You are being cagey. What is going on?"

"He is unaware of the nature of the mission."

"And it is dangerous?"

Casimir didn't respond, but a slight twitch near his left eye made me suspect I had hit on something significant.

"Don't get yourself killed."

Genuine surprise flickered in his eyes. Green and changeable like my betrothed, they were also very different. There was a guarded hardness to Casimir that Illeron lacked. It made me want to give him a hug. He needed affection, someone to soften that shell.

"I have no intention of dying," he pointed out dryly.

"Good." I crossed the space and wrapped my arms around him. He stiffened awkwardly. "Accept it, Casimir. You are family, and I care." Then, taking pity on the elf, I released him. Backing away immediately, I met his confused expression with a slight smile. "Come back to us."

"I will." The two words so gravely spoken weighed heavily in the air between us. He opened his mouth as though prepared to say more. But at the last moment, he shook his head and chose to bow instead. "Be well, Avril."

"And you, Casimir." He was gone before I spoke his name.

Something in my gut told me it would be a long while before I saw him again.

Casimir returns in
The Shadow Elf's Rescuer
Elves of Eldarlan - Book Two

THE SHADOW ELF'S RESCUER

Elves of Eldarlan - Book Two

In a world full of elves, woodwose, gargoyles, and brownies, shadow elves are the most feared. Casimir, brother of the elven king's spymaster, has become well acquainted with that reviling in his years of service to his brother and his king. Now, dying slowly at the hands of a crazed magus, he holds out no hope of rescue. Who would risk their life for a nightmare like him?

Veta lives to protect her younger half-brother, so when a village raid demands immediate action, she exchanges her life for his. Dragged into a magus' horrifying workroom in the depths of his fortress, she comes face to face with a nightmare, a shadow elf. However, tortured and dying, he clearly poses no danger. That is until he offers her a bargain.

Writing as Elisa Rae

The Elven Spymaster's Thief
The Shadow Elf's Rescuer
(coming soon)
The Elf King's Sacrifice
(coming soon)

Writing as Rachel Rossano

Once Upon a Duchy
(Novels Inspired by Fairy Tales)
Grace by Contract
Reclaiming Ryda
Rumpled Rhett

Novels of Rhynan
(Medieval Romances)
Duty
Honor
Mercy
Making of a Man
(a short story anthology)

The Talented
(Inspirational Fantasy)
Seventh Born
The Defender
Living Sacrifice

About the Author

A reader of fairytales and folklore, Elisa Rae loves a happy ending. Noblebright characters, dastardly villains, and chemistry between characters delight her. When she isn't writing, she loves to watch superhero movies and literary dramas.

If you like romantic adventures of various kinds, join her at: https://www.rachelrossano.com/elisa-rae!

To keep up with her literary adventures, feel free to follow her on Amazon (https://www.amazon.com/Elisa-Rae/e/B09NV5XYMV) or check out her Facebook page (https://www.facebook.com/ElisaRaeAuthor).

She is also active on Instagram (https://www.instagram.com/anavrea/)

www.ingramcontent.com/pod-product-compliance
Ingram Content Group UK Ltd.
Pitfield, Milton Keynes, MK11 3LW, UK
UKHW040007200726
13854UKWH00001B/90